THE RECKLESS SEVEN

THE MACMILLAN COMPANY
NEW YORK · BOSTON · CHICAGO · DALLAS
ATLANTA · SAN FRANCISCO

MACMILLAN & CO., Limited
LONDON · BOMBAY · CALCUTTA
MELBOURNE

THE MACMILLAN COMPANY
OF CANADA, Limited
TORONTO

Mr. Bailey burst in on his family.

THE RECKLESS SEVEN

BY
NELLY RIEU

Illustrated by
ELOISE BURNS

NEW YORK
THE MACMILLAN COMPANY
1930

SET UP BY BROWN BROTHERS LINOTYPERS
PRINTED IN THE UNITED STATES OF AMERICA
BY THE FERRIS PRINTING COMPANY

CONTENTS

CHAPTER		PAGE
I.	THE ARRIVAL IN ALDERNEY	1
II.	HOME, SWEET HOME	13
III.	THE SEVEN LOST	41
IV.	THE SEVEN FOUND	60
V.	THE FIRST PICNIC	73
VI.	THE PLEASURES OF RABBITING	93
VII.	THE DESERTED ISLAND	108
VIII.	THE STORM RISES	124
IX.	CASTAWAY COTTAGE	139
X.	HARD WORK	163
XI.	A SURPRISE FROM THE BLUE	181
XII.	THE THIRD CAVE	196
XIII.	TREASURE TROVE	214
XIV.	THE ARRIVAL OF ROBERT	236
XV.	OLD NED'S NEST-EGG	256
XVI.	A HAPPY MEETING	277

ILLUSTRATIONS

Mr. Bailey burst in on his family . . . . . . *Frontispiece*

PAGE

"Oh, what a wonderful place!" exclaimed Rose . . . 17

"It's a terrible place!" said the woman 21

The gate opened with a loud grating noise 25

At last the hands marked the half hour 87

Mr. Bailey smoked a peaceful pipe 113

They were castaways in real earnest 147

They peered half fearfully into the cave 199

THE RECKLESS SEVEN

Charles

CHAPTER I

THE ARRIVAL IN ALDERNEY

"WHAT delicious eggs and bacon!" cried Mr. Bailey happily. "And Oxford marmalade! This is a splendid hotel."

"It's a delightful place," agreed Mrs. Bailey. "How glad I am to be here at last!"

The Seven were silent. They had begun their breakfast.

It was their first morning on the island that had filled their thoughts for many weeks past; yet already their old home in the little house in St. John's Wood, and all London with it, seemed to belong to the land of dreams. Here was a new world, separated from the old by an adventurous journey over land and sea—a new world of clear sunshine, in which the sea that lay stretched below their window sparkled and shone. There by the jetty they could see the tramp steamer, now looking incredibly small, that had brought them from Littlehampton and, only last night, landed them here in Alderney. Now it was being loaded with its cargo of stone from the quarry close by, ready for its return journey. The noise of a busy little crane came to them through the open window, and trucks running to and fro along miniature railway lines added a lively interest to the scene.

Perhaps the best and quickest way of introducing the Seven is to quote a verse recently written by William who, amidst derisive cheers from the rest, had once acclaimed himself Poet Laureate of the family:

> Charles, fourteen, is fair of face,
> Will, thirteen, does nothing base,
> Rosie, twelve, is worldly-wise,
> Violet, ten, just sits and sighs,
> Stella, nine, is quite a star,
> Tony, seven, says "There you are!"
> Maurice, six, can scarcely mount
> A rocking-horse, so doesn't count.

"What a silly poem!" exclaimed Charles, when William first recited these lines to the family.

"Yes, and I won't be called 'Rosie'," protested Rose. "It makes me sound idiotic."

"My dear Rose," said the poet in a hurt voice, "if I have added a syllable to your name I have taken one from mine, so it's all square. And have you never heard of poetic license? And don't you know that all the best poetry has to scan? I will recite it to you again, and you will see how trippingly the lines run."

"If you do," threatened Charles, "I will punch your head."

"Oh, Charles!" intervened Mrs. Bailey, in her sweet, slightly pained voice. "I think it's a very nice poem, and he has all your ages quite right."

"He could have done that in prose," said Charles. "There's no need to make a song about it."

"But I couldn't have got the names and ages *and* the characters of seven people into eight lines of prose," retorted William. "It would have taken eight pages. That's the great advantage of poetry. It's so concise."

"Character!" scoffed Charles. "What have you said about my character?"

"Nothing!" said his brother. "That's why it's so true."

They had always lived in London, though never for long in the same house. Charles and William had dim memories of a mansion peopled with servants and nurses. As a matter of fact the mansion had been a tall, narrow house in a quiet square, with two maids and one nurse. Then, as the family grew larger and Mr. Bailey's income remained about the same, house after house grew smaller, and the staff dwindled to one maid-of-all-work.

Yet through all the changing fortunes of the family two things remained firm: one was Mr. Bailey's happy confidence in the future prosperity of his family through the success that would one day crown his literary work; the other was Mrs. Bailey's unshakable conviction that her husband was the best and wisest man in the world.

Then came the time for yet another move. Rents were higher, and houses to let scarcer than ever before, and even Mr. Bailey's good spirits became damped by long and fruitless house-hunting.

"I have wasted three months, interviewing impossible house agents and looking at still more impossible houses," he said one day, as he sat down to lunch after a tiring and disappointing expedition to a distant suburb. "My work is at a standstill. My publishers are worrying me for the last chapter of my book on 'Primitive Peoples,' which I promised them last month and have not yet been able to finish. I am beginning to wish I were a Primitive Man myself, with a good, roomy cave to live in, and no rent to pay."

"We have too many children," sighed his wife. "All the house agents say so. But something must be done. We promised to leave this house in March, and now it is June, and poor Mrs. Pine is waiting to come into it."

"Let her pine and go to Pinner, while we stay here and eat our dinner," murmured William, hoping to give the conversation a brighter turn.

"Silence, boy!" thundered his father. "This is no joking matter. Well, Alice," he continued, turning to his wife, "something must be done, as you say, and I have come to the conclusion that we must look farther afield, though the thought of leaving London depresses me. In fact, if we have to leave it, I should like to go so far away that I could forget it altogether, and I think we might do worse than that place in Alderney I was telling you about."

"Oh, Arthur!" exclaimed his wife. "You didn't tell me anything, or if you did I wasn't listening. I thought you were joking."

"There are some things I never joke about, and house-hunting is one of them," said Mr. Bailey, a smile breaking through the unwonted gloom of his face. "I'll tell you again. It was Black who told me about it. He's the great authority on Roman coins, you know. I met him yesterday at the Club, and told him of the trouble we were having. He said what a pity it was that things were always in the wrong places, and that in Alderney, where he went last year for his holiday, you could get a disused fort, with acres of ground, for a mere song. He thought they —for there are at least half-a-dozen of them now empty—would make delightful dwelling houses for large families."

"Do you think it's true, Arthur?" asked Mrs. Bailey doubtfully. In her struggles with housekeeping she had long ago given up the hope of getting anything for a song.

"I don't know; but I'll find out. Children, how would you like to live in a fort?"

A shout of approval went up from the Seven.

"Of course the children would like it," said their

mother; "but do you think that we should? I have heard of Alderney; but I know nothing at all about it."

"Nor do I," confessed Mr. Bailey, "except that it is one of the Channel Islands, noted for cows. Charles, get me an atlas."

Charles made a dash for the bookcase, and a storm of comments and questions broke loose.

"An island—surrounded by water!"

"May we bathe every day?"

"Can we have a boat?"

"May I have a cow of my own?"

"Are there any people on it?"

"Are they black?"

"Be quiet, children," cried Mr. Bailey. "Your mother is speaking and I can't hear what she says."

"I want to know if there are any schools there," said Mrs. Bailey.

"Oh, Mother!" groaned Charles. "What a question to ask!"

Mr. Bailey looked doubtful.

"Well," he said in a hesitating voice, "there must be a school of some sort there, because Black said it has a population of over 1,000; but if it isn't a suitable one the children might continue their studies under my supervision for a time."

It was Mrs. Bailey's turn to look doubtful.

"Anyhow, it would only be for a year or two," continued her husband more cheerfully. "By that time the royalties on my new book will enable us to send them all to good schools. But don't let us worry about anything before it's necessary. We may never go to Alderney, though I must say that, on the map, it looks very attractive."

"It looks very small," said Mrs. Bailey, looking over his shoulder at the atlas.

"About four miles long by two miles broad, I should say, roughly. I must get an ordnance map —something on a bigger scale than this—before we can see any details. I'll find out more about it at once. I'll go to Whitehall straight away, and try to track down the department that deals in old forts. Children, my hat and gloves!"

He rose briskly from the table, and the children flew to do his bidding. Five minutes later they were all at the door, waving him out of sight.

Once Mr. Bailey's interest was aroused he followed his quest with untiring zeal. Had he been an explorer, or a general at the head of some perilous expedition, he would have been entirely happy and, probably, have achieved greatness. The forts of Alderney fired his imagination. The more he heard about them the greater became his determination to possess one. For the next few days he was deep in negotiations to that end, and every difficulty that presented itself in the way of transporting his large family he overcame with masterly skill. All Mrs. Bailey's doubts were set at rest by his pictures of a life spent in happy security, free from bustle and worry and unpaid bills, with perfect health for the children, and for himself long, uninterrupted days in which he could give himself up to writing. It ended in his coming home one day with full permission to occupy the fort of his choice at a rental that was little more than nominal.

"I've got one at last!" he announced triumphantly, bursting in on his family as they sat at tea.

"Got one what?" asked his wife, who was busy cutting bread and spreading on jam.

"A fort, of course. It's all settled. Built in the reign of good Queen Victoria to protect us from our friends the French, and now let to Mr. Arthur Montgomery Bailey, the well-known writer on Primitive Man and His Times."

"Oh, Arthur!" cried Mrs. Bailey. "Have you really done it?"

"I have. We now have a home waiting for us. No more house-hunting! When can you be ready?"

"The children's schools break up in a fortnight's time, and I may be able to finish packing by then. I suppose the furniture people will see to the furniture packing?"

"Of course. The next thing is to find out the best and cheapest way of getting to our island. I'll fix that up as soon as possible. I shan't be able to settle down to my work till we are in our new home."

"You won't forget that we have decided to have a tutor for the children, will you?" asked Mrs. Bailey anxiously, amid groans from the Seven.

"I am going to write tonight to my old tutor at Oxford. He always knows of some young genius on the look-out for work or adventure."

"He will probably get both with us," said Mrs. Bailey hopefully. "He can come to us in September, after the summer holidays. We shall be well settled in by then."

The next fortnight was a glorious time of picnic meals and constant excitement for the Seven. When they learned that they were to make the journey by sea in a tramp steamer their cup of happiness was full.

"It's a remarkable looking old tub—but very safe, the captain says," their father announced. "They call it a stone-boat."

"How can a stone-boat float?" asked Stella anxiously.

"It's a wooden boat that brings stone from Alderney, where there are quarries. It spends all its time in running to and fro between there and Littlehampton, where we shall have to embark."

"Where shall we sleep?" asked Rose.

"Oh, somewhere down in the hold, I expect," said her father teasingly. "The captain says you'll make splendid ballast."

"I don't mind where we sleep," said Mrs. Bailey. "The comfort is that, once on board, we stay there till we are landed on our island."

"And our furniture with us," added her husband.

"I wish we were starting today," sighed Charles, voicing the sentiments of the Seven. "Or else I wish I could go to sleep now, and wake up on the day when we set out to sea."

> "Even the weariest river
> Winds somewhere safe to sea,"

quoted William soothingly.

"That's a comforting thought, certainly," said Mrs. Bailey with a smile. "I'll keep it in mind as I do the packing. But I don't think that any of you children know what weariness is."

"Nor do rivers," declared Charles stoutly. "Anyone but a poet would know that they enjoy traveling, and hate hanging about getting ready to start."

Whatever the feelings of rivers may be, the Seven certainly enjoyed every minute of the journey to the sea, and on the sea, and there were no signs of weariness on the happy faces gathered round that first breakfast at the journey's end.

CHAPTER II

HOME, SWEET HOME

"MAY we go to the Fort directly we have finished?" asked Charles as they reached the marmalade stage of their breakfast.

"Yes," said his father. "I am going to walk there, and you and William, and Rose, and Stella can come with me. I've ordered a car to be sent round for your mother and the younger ones, as I'm sure they would rather drive."

"We would," agreed Mrs. Bailey. "We'll bring some of the smaller luggage with us. And I'll order some sandwiches, and we'll have a picnic there."

"Mayn't we sleep there tonight?" asked William anxiously.

"Oh, do please let us," implored the rest.

"It depends on what time the furniture turns up, and on how long it takes to unload it," said Mr. Bailey. "If we can get the place ready we'll certainly sleep there."

"Hurrah!" shouted the Seven.

"This hotel is awfully nice," added Charles; "but I expect the Fort will be more fun."

Half an hour later Mr. Bailey and the four elder children stood on the doorstep, ready to set out.

"I'll follow you very soon," promised Mrs. Bailey. "I have a little shopping to do first."

"Shopping already!" cried her husband with a laugh. "What ever can you want to buy in this remote island?"

"You will know at lunch-time," said Mrs. Bailey. "I must get a few groceries, too."

"Yes, I suppose we shall want them," agreed her husband resignedly. "But remember that the caretaker at the Fort keeps a cow, and fowls, so we may be able to get butter and eggs from him. And come along as soon as you can."

With a parting wave of his hat he set out with the four elder children. A map of the island, which had been his constant companion for the past two or three weeks, was open in his hand, and he studied it closely as they went along.

"We go straight up to the Butes," he said, "and then drop down the hillside to the bay below, and walk along the shore till we come to our Fort."

"Oh, what a wonderful place!" exclaimed Rose, as they stood for a moment on the hill and looked down on to the harbor. "What is that wall going straight out to sea?"

"That's a breakwater. I should like to see the sea come dashing over it."

"Do you think it's ever very rough here?" asked William, as they took the grassy footpath down the steep slope to the shore. "It looks now as if it were going to be calm for ever."

"You needn't worry about that," said his father. "The seas here are tremendous, and in a gale I doubt if you would be able to stand upright on this hill. They tell me that the boat that brings the mails twice or three times a week from Guernsey, and incidentally supplies all the outside wants of the islanders, is often held up for several days at a time in rough weather. Even in fine weather it needs skilful piloting, because of the strong currents and outlying rocks."

"May we paddle along to our Fort?" asked Rose eagerly as they reached the shore.

"That's just what I am going to do," said her father, sitting down on the fine shingle and beginning to take off his boots. "Our Fort is at the end of the next bay, and we shall see it directly we round that corner."

The quarter of an hour that followed was full of wild joy to children who had not been to the seaside for nearly a year. In the pleasures of getting wet and finding wonderful specimens of shells and seaweed they almost forgot their destination. Only Mr. Bailey paddled steadily on. But by dint of occasional flying dashes they all managed to arrive at the end of the bay together.

"Now we'll keep to the cart-track along the shore under the hill," said Mr. Bailey. "It would take us all the morning to climb over the rocks."

Once on the grass-grown road they all broke into a run to see which would get the first glimpse of their new home. As they rounded the corner they burst into loud cheers. Before them stretched another beautiful bay, with wild rocks at its farther end, from which rose the frowning circular walls of a fortification.

"What a wonderful place to live in!" they all ejaculated in various keys of delight.

With their eyes fixed on the Fort ahead they hardly noticed the steep slopes that came down to the flat, green track along which they trotted, and the wild flowers that grew all around were passed

"Oh, what a wonderful place!" exclaimed Rose.

unheeded. Grazing by the wayside were many tethered cows, and halfway round the bay was a lonely, weather-beaten cottage.

A woman and a small boy came to the door to look at them. Mr. Bailey was so happy that he felt he must stop and tell them the wonderful news.

"We're going to that Fort," he shouted joyously, pointing to it with his stick. "We shall be neighbors."

The woman came nearer, as if to get a better view of such strange beings.

"Ah!" she exclaimed in a tone of hushed amazement. "Then you must be the gentleman from London that's taken the Fort."

"Makes me sound like the hero of some great naval victory," cried Mr. Bailey delightedly. "You're quite right. We're going to live there."

"It's a terrible place," she said sourly.

"Terrible!" echoed Mr. Bailey, looking suddenly very crestfallen. "I call it the most beautiful place in the world."

The woman shook her head.

"Wait till you've lived here for twenty winters, as I've done," she sighed, "then maybe you'll think differently."

"And what about the twenty summers?" he demanded with some heat. "Surely they must have made up for a great deal."

"It's the winters I think most about," said the woman, who was obviously not one who had ever dwelt on the bright side of things. "With the sea dashing over the rocks, and the currents running something cruel, and the wild wind howling, and never a soul in sight, and——"

"Ah, that will all be altered now," interrupted Mr. Bailey briskly as soon as he saw an opening for stemming the tide of her complaints. "You'll see plenty of us. But now we must be getting along. Come, children, or your mother will arrive before us."

They stepped out briskly, and soon came to the farther headland of the bay, where great masses of rock jutted out into the sea, ending in a low, flat-topped giant on which the Fort was built. A rough causeway of stone slabs, with rocks and sea on either side, led out to it.

"In those terrible winters of which we have heard, the Fort must be completely cut off from the mainland at high tide," remarked Mr. Bailey cheerfully. "I must say that I look forward to living on a little island of our own."

"It's a terrible place!" said the woman.

They walked along the causeway and approached a small iron door set in the high, circular, outer walls of the Fort. The stone flags ended abruptly on the edge of a deep moat that ran round the wall, over which was laid a narrow bridge of planks. They crossed the bridge and tried the door. It was locked fast. They stood on the threshold of their new home, and knocked.

"I hope that the caretaker and his wife are not out," said Mr. Bailey anxiously. "They ought to be here to receive us; but the whole place looks deserted. We'll give them a shout."

They all shouted together. A grille in the door opened with a sudden, unearthly screech that made them jump, and a pair of bright brown eyes regarded them suspiciously through the bars.

"Please open the door and let us in," said Mr. Bailey in a bold voice, though he felt a shiver of dismay go down his spine. "My name is Bailey. I was told that you would expect us today."

There was a long fumbling at many bolts, and then the door slowly opened, with a loud grating noise that sounded like groan.

Before them stood an elderly man, wearing an old blue jersey pulled down over a pair of flannel trousers that were rolled up to his knees. Brown sand-shoes and a red woollen scarf completed his outfit. His tanned and weather-beaten face was half hidden by a gray, scrubby beard.

"A pirate!" whispered William in Charles' ear.

"We heard you was coming," said the apparition in a deep, gruff voice; "but we thought that it was most likely some mistake."

"There's no mistake," said Mr. Bailey firmly. "Our furniture will be here this morning, and we are anxious to settle in at once."

"You're the first that's ever wanted to do that in all the years we've been here. It's a terribly lonesome place."

"I'm sorry you think so," said Mr. Bailey, trying to speak pleasantly. "I hoped that you and your wife would stay on here, and look after us."

"Well—we might, and we mightn't. I don't know what Matilda will say. Matilda!" he shouted in a roar that startled the little group before him, "Matilda! Here is the gentleman what's taken the Fort."

As he shouted he led the way across a courtyard overgrown with grass and weeds, in which a few fowls were scraping up a living. Mr. Bailey and

The gate opened with a loud grating noise.

the children followed him silently. None of them had ever before seen the inside of a fort. They had pictured it vaguely as a romantic stronghold, full of associations derived from stories of high adventure. The desolate solitude of this fort, long forsaken and purposeless, took them by surprise, and filled them with sudden awe. Without life of its own, and cut off from the life of the outer world by its gray, un-scalable walls, it seemed a place apart, peopled by ghosts from the past.

The voice of their guide rang out hoarsely, and died down in strange echoes. Before them a second massive iron door, in the inner wall of the building, opened slowly, and a woman peered out.

"Here, Matilda," again shouted the man. "Here's the gentleman what's taken the Fort."

Matilda opened the door wide, and came into full view.

She looks rather like a fort herself, thought Mr. Bailey.

She was a tall, bony woman, with hair and complexion very much the color of the surrounding walls. Unlike her husband, she was extremely neat, and her voice when she spoke was surprisingly soft.

"Will you be wanting lunch, sir?" she asked

the children followed him silently. None of them
had ever before seen the inside of a fort. They had
pictured it vaguely as a romantic stronghold, full of
associations derived from stories of high adventure.
The desolate solitude of this fort, long forsaken and
purposeless, took them by surprise, and filled them
with sudden awe. Without life of its own, and cut
off from the life of the outer world by its gray, un-
scalable walls, it seemed a place apart, peopled by
ghosts from the past.

The voice of their guide rang out hoarsely, and
died down in strange echoes. Before them a second
massive iron door, in the inner wall of the building,
opened slowly, and a woman peered out.

"Here, Matilda," again shouted the man. "Here's
the gentleman what's taken the Fort."

Matilda opened the door wide, and came into full
view.

"She looks rather like a fort herself," thought Mr.
Bailey.

She was a tall, bony woman, with hair and complexion very much the color of the surrounding walls.
Unlike her husband, she was extremely neat, and her
voice when she spoke was surprisingly soft.

"Will you be wanting lunch, sir?" she asked.

Mr. Bailey was so taken aback by this simple but unexpected question that for a moment or so he was speechless. He would have been much less surprised had she ordered him out of the Fort!

"Er—yes—no," he stuttered. "No, thank you, my wife is coming almost at once, and is bringing our lunch with her. We prepared for a picnic—we did not expect that you would be able to supply us with a meal at such short notice. As a matter of fact," he went on quickly, thinking it well to get over the worst at once, "we have seven children."

He looked at her anxiously, as he had so often looked at the house-agents in London when he made this announcement. He half expected her to say that she would start packing at once. Instead she smiled, in a pitying way.

"Only seven!" she said sadly. "I had thirteen. I've lost them all."

"Lost them all!" repeated Mr. Bailey in a tone out of which he could not keep his dismay. His gaze went quickly to his own four silent children, who stood spellbound round the door.

"That's her way of speaking," broke in the man, frowning and shaking his head vigorously at his wife. "They've all grown up and gone to foreign parts."

Mr. Bailey was greatly relieved. "I was afraid they were all dead," he said.

"It's the same thing," replied Matilda mournfully. "I wish you had thirteen. Seven will be lost in this Fort."

Later on Mr. Bailey was to remember these ominous words with a feeling of chill horror. But now he answered cheerfully enough.

"Oh, no, I hope not. I mean that I think we shall find them enough. We came on ahead to let you know that we had arrived. We will go back now to meet the rest of the family. Come along, children."

With a smile and a nod he turned and retraced his steps across the courtyard, the children rushing helter-skelter before him. Once outside the enclosure of those forbidding walls their high spirits returned with a bound.

"Phew!" exclaimed Mr. Bailey, mopping his brow, though the morning was fresh and cool. "What an amazing place!"

"I hope Mummy will like it," cried Charles, voicing his father's thought. "I wish she would hurry up."

"Frightened by the pirate, weren't you?" asked William teasingly. "I saw you turn pale."

"Do you think he is a real pirate?" asked Violet anxiously.

"Of course he is. Didn't you see his muffler—dyed red with the blood of his victims?"

"Here's Mother coming," interposed Rose joyfully.

A car was rounding the rocks at the end of the bay, coming slowly toward them along the rough track.

"We'll go to meet them," said Mr. Bailey, setting out along the causeway at a quick pace.

They reached the shore as the car drew up, and the children began eagerly to pour out their news to the newcomers.

"Oh, Mummy, a real pirate!"

"With a red scarf, like a pirate in a book!"

"He says it's a terribly lonely place!"

"Be quiet a moment, children," cried their father. "Here, boys, help Maurice out, and take these baskets. My dear, what a lot of luggage you have brought!"

"I brought it all. The captain called to say that

he had sent our furniture off, and that it would be here before us, so I told the people at the hotel that we should not be returning there. And I bought a few stores, too."

Mr. Bailey groaned as he thought of the homely comfort of the hotel. "The furniture hasn't arrived yet," he said, "and I really think we had better go back to the hotel for a day or two at least."

"But think of the expense, Arthur!" exclaimed his wife. "How pale you look! Aren't you feeling well? Oh dear, I hope you're not sickening for anything!"

"Don't worry about me. I've had measles and whooping-cough, and all the things that one sickens for." He tried to speak in a light and bantering tone; but his wife still looked at him anxiously.

"Well, come indoors, dear. Have you seen the caretakers yet? We must go and arrange where our furniture is to go before it arrives. And is there a store-cupboard?"

"Store-cupboard?" repeated her husband, as if he had never heard of such a thing, so far away were his thoughts. "I really didn't notice; in fact, I haven't noticed anything yet. We haven't been inside the building—we were waiting for you."

"Then come along, and let us explore our new home together," said Mrs. Bailey briskly. "Maurice, you take Daddy's hand. Children, help with the parcels."

"Shall I bring up the big parcels, ma'am?" asked the man who had driven them out. His offer was not made altogether out of kindness. He felt a lively interest in the new tenants of the Fort, and was more than curious to see their first entry.

"That's very good of you," said Mrs. Bailey, "I shall be very glad if you will."

They unpacked the car, and all went up the causeway, staggering under loads of many shapes and sizes.

"I'm just beginning to understand Noah's feelings when he entered the Ark," said Mr. Bailey. "The Noah family probably looked very much like ours."

"What did Noah wear?" asked Tony.

"I'll tell you tonight when you're in bed. I'm too busy now."

"I love our front drive," said Mrs. Bailey, looking round at the sea and rocks. "I expect there's not another like it in the world."

"And here is our front door," said her husband. He tried to push it open. It was again fast shut.

For the second time that morning he stood outside

his Fort and shouted. For the second time a pair of bright brown eyes looked at him suspiciously through the little iron grille before the door was opened to him.

"Is it necessary to keep this place barred and bolted?" he asked, with a touch of annoyance in his voice. "You knew we were coming back again."

"It's the fowls," said the man sadly. "Matilda don't like them straying about all over the place. I got to keep 'em in somehow."

"Ah yes, of course," said Mr. Bailey, feeling that he had spoken too hastily. "I never thought of the fowls. By the way, what is your name?'

"Robert Lecoke," said the man.

"A very interesting name—one that I do not remember to have heard before. How do you spell it?"

"R-o-b——"

"No, no," interrupted Mr. Bailey. "I meant your second name, Lecoke."

"L-e-c-o-q," slowly spelt out the owner of the name.

"Ah, yes, a long 'o,' of course," mused Mr. Bailey. "It's curious how——"

"Arthur, dear," interrupted his wife, "do let us go in. I am longing to see our new house, and you will have plenty of time to discuss place-names when we are settled down."

"Place-names!" protested her husband. "I was not——"

"No, I know, dear; but never mind now. May we call you Robert?" she asked, turning to the care-taker. "I think it's such a splendid name."

Robert looked pleased. He smiled for the first time since the family had arrived, and nodded his consent.

"And now we must make haste," she continued, "or the furniture will be here before we have had time to look round."

The procession struggled on across the courtyard, with Robert leading the way, shouting loudly for Matilda until her grim figure again appeared in the doorway.

"Good-morning, Matilda," said Mrs. Bailey, with her pleasant smile. "We have come. If you will show us the store-cupboard we will get rid of these parcels before you take us round the house."

Without a word Matilda turned and led the way indoors. Evidently she was a silent woman, or per-haps the solitude of her surroundings had overcome any desire for speech. The little party followed her into a high, bare entrance hall, and along a gray stone corridor lit by narrow windows placed high up in the thick walls.

"It's very cold here," said Mrs. Bailey, with a shiver.

Matilda turned. "It's always cold here," she said gravely. "Cold in summer, and colder in winter."

Mrs. Bailey looked dismayed. She hated the cold.

"We'll have splendid roaring fires," said her husband in tones of forced cheerfulness.

"And we'll roast chestnuts," cried William, and all the Seven at once found their tongues at the thought of this homely occupation, and the gray stone corridors echoed with their voices.

Matilda stopped at last before another closed iron door, turned the enormous rusty key that was in the lock, and flung it wide.

"The store-cupboard," she announced.

"Oh, what a lovely room to play robbers in!" shouted Anthony.

"Or Ali Baba and the Forty Thieves," said Violet. "You could easily get forty-one people in here, couldn't you, Daddy?"

"Oh, easily," said Mr. Bailey. "And plenty of room for the stores as well."

"Oh, Arthur!" cried Mrs. Bailey. "It looks more like a vault than a store-cupboard. How ever shall we keep it clean?"

"This isn't London, you know," replied her husband soothingly. "There's no dust flying about."

The parcels were all laid on the floor just inside the door, and Mr. Bailey dropped a tip into the hand of the man who had driven out the car and so obligingly carried in the heavier packages.

"If you meet the furniture," he said, "tell the men to hurry up."

"All right," replied the man. "And if you want a motor-boat at any time I have a beauty I can let you have—by the name of *Saucy Sally*. My name is Mr. James. Robert can tell you where I live."

"Oh, what fun!" cried the children. "Do let's have it, Daddy."

"Later on, perhaps," said their father. "Thank you, Mr. James. I won't forget, and when we want a boat I'll let you know."

Mr. James clumped away down the corridor, accompanied by Robert.

"Would you like to see the other rooms now?" asked Matilda. "Though when you've seen one you've seen them all," she added glumly. "They're all alike."

"We should like to see them all, please," said Mrs. Bailey firmly. "I don't think I like her much," she added in a whisper to her husband, as they all trooped off again.

"She's not exactly winsome," he whispered back; "but under that frowning exterior may beat a heart of gold."

"Perhaps," she answered doubtfully. "What a lovely big room!" she exclaimed aloud, as Matilda flung open the door of a huge dining-hall.

"They're all *big*," said Matilda, emphasizing the one adjective to show her disagreement with the other. She stalked on again, throwing open several more doors.

"I must buy some oil for these locks at the very first opportunity," said Mr. Bailey. "I can't stand their creaking and screeching. It reminds me of a prison."

"What is prison like, Daddy?" asked Violet eagerly. "Is it really anything like this?"

"Don't they oil the doors in a prison?" asked Stella.

"I expect they let them get rusty to annoy the prisoners," said Rose.

"They always go about clanking the keys, too," added William. "Don't they, Daddy?"

"Now look here, children, if you think I'm going

to be drawn into a discussion of prison life—of which, by the way, I know no more than you do—you are mistaken. Now this is a nice room. I think I shall have it for my study."

"I think Matilda is right," said Mrs. Bailey, "they all look very much alike—so big and bare."

"That's because the windows are so high and so small that you get no view," said her husband. "When we are living in them they will be very different. We'll go round them again and settle where our furniture is to go. Children, you can all go out into the courtyard and play."

"May we paddle?" asked Charles.

"Not before lunch," said his father. "It's nearly twelve o'clock now."

"Just play about here," said Mrs. Bailey, as she led them back to the courtyard. "Charles, you look after Maurice—and William, you see to Stella and Anthony. We won't be long, and I have a lovely lunch for you, and we will go out and sit on the rocks while we eat it."

"Are there bananas for lunch?" asked Maurice eagerly.

"Bananas *and* eggs," said Mrs. Bailey, "and chocolate to finish up with. So be very good."

"We'll play at robbers," said Charles.

"Can we all be robbers?" asked Tony doubtfully.

"Yes, of course, all of us in turn."

"Children have curious ideas of being good," remarked Mr. Bailey, as he and his wife went back into the building to discuss ways and means. "Where are Robert and Matilda? They seem to have disappeared."

"Thank goodness," said his wife. "They depress me. They take such a gloomy view of this place as a home."

"Well, they've lived in it for the last ten years themselves, so I think it should be possible for us to live here for one or two. They have been too much alone, I expect, and have got a bit rusty. We'll soon liven them up. Which room would you like for the nursery?"

They soon became so deeply interested in making plans for their new home that they never noticed how time was passing. At last Mr. Bailey looked at his watch and gave an exclamation of surprise.

"It's after one o'clock," he said. "The furniture ought to have been here long ago. And those children will be starving. Let's get the picnic basket, and have lunch at once."

They went to the storeroom for the basket, and were quickly at the front door. There was no one in sight.

"Children," shouted Mr. Bailey, "lunch-time!"

He went out and glanced all round the still and overgrown courtyard. No sign of life met his eye. Even the fowls had retired to a corner, and lay basking drowsily in a patch of sunlight.

"Children, children!" he shouted again.

There was no answering cry from the Seven.

William

CHAPTER III

THE SEVEN LOST

FOR a long time after Mr. and Mrs. Bailey had left them the children played happily at their game of robbers. All round the main building was a grass-grown passage; and some small outbuildings and miniature embankments made splendid shelter from which most effective and exciting raids could be made. Maurice wanted to be a robber all the time, and Anthony refused to put his hands up when ordered to do so with a pistol pointing at his head; but apart from a few such minor hitches the game went on vigorously till robbers and robbed were tired out, and lay resting on the ground.

41

"I want to go indoors to Mummy now," announced Maurice.

"Mummy is busy; come with me for a little walk, and I'll show you something wonderful," said Charles in his most persuasive voice. "You must stay with us till lunch-time."

"Let's go on a treasure hunt," suggested William.

The Seven forgot that they had ever felt tired, and all jumped up, eager to set out on this new expedition.

"We'll keep together," said Charles, "so that we can all find the treasure at the same time, and divide it up equally between us. Maurice, you hold my hand."

"And Anthony, you come with me," ordered William.

"We'll walk round under the walls," said Violet, "and pretend we are soldiers who have just won a great victory, and taken the Fort from the robbers."

"And we'll hunt round to see that no enemy is in hiding, waiting to shoot us down from behind when we take off our armor and sit down to the feast that is preparing," said William.

"Am I a soldier, too?" asked Anthony.

"Yes, of course," Charles assured him. "You're a captain."

"What am I?" asked Maurice.

"You're a sergeant-major. Now come along—
left, right, left, right."

They marched along under the walls that pro-
tected the Fort from the sea, peering into odd corners,
and looking for robbers and treasure by turn, till
Stella spied the iron door to an outhouse, half-
hidden by a low-growing bush.

"Perhaps robbers are hiding in there," she whispered, stopping before it, while the others gathered
round.

"Open it," said William. "We'll soon put them
to rout."

"There's no handle or key to it," said Charles. "I
expect it's locked. Which way does it open?"

"Inwards," declared William, examining it with
the professional eye of an amateur carpenter.

"Then we'll put our shoulders to it, and push together, William."

The two boys pushed with all their might; but the
door did not budge.

"Wants oiling," said William. "I don't expect it's
been open for years."

"Let's all push together," said Rose. "You boys
push the door, and we'll push you."

The Seven thought this great fun, and threw themselves at the door, and at each other, with all their might. After many united efforts the door swung suddenly open, without any warning, and the three elder ones fell headlong forward, with the rest on top of them.

They picked themselves and each other up, and the "babies," as the younger ones were patronizingly called by their elders, were comforted and brushed down, and assured that no bones were broken and no blood spilt. Then they all peered curiously through the now open door. They saw a small, bare room, square and empty.

"A good thing it wasn't full of robbers," said Rose.

"And a good thing it wasn't a deep pit or an old well, or we should all have fallen in and perished," laughed Charles.

"What do you think it's meant for?" asked William, going into the room and looking round.

"Perhaps the robbers kept their gunpowder there," suggested Violet.

"Or perhaps they kept their prisoners there, and tortured them," added Charles in a blood-curdling whisper.

Maurice began to cry. He was getting tired and hungry.

"I only said that for fun," said Charles, giving him a reassuring pat on the back. "I think it was for storing gunpowder, or coal—or bags of money. You come in with me, and have a look round. Perhaps we'll find a secret spring in the wall, and when you press it you'll see a hole full of gold and silver and diamonds."

Maurice was all smiles and excitement at once, and in another moment the Seven were inside, feeling carefully over the walls for hidden springs, as high as they could reach.

"Perhaps there's a hollow place in the floor, and a trapdoor," said William.

"And steps leading on to the shore, that the robbers used when they brought their stolen treasures home," suggested Rose.

"Or a well down which they threw the dead bodies of their prisoners," said William. "We may find a few skeletons if we look long enough."

"Shut up!" warned Charles, looking anxiously at Maurice. But Maurice was now too interested to be disturbed by the alarming conversation of his elders.

"There's no window," said Rose. "It must be quite dark in here when the door's shut."

"I'll shut it and see," said William.

"Shut it and *not* see, you mean," corrected Violet.

"Very clever!" scoffed William, as he took hold of the door and gently pushed it to. "There's still a little light. Where do you think it comes from, Charles?"

"The door isn't quite shut. If it were it would be pitch dark, because there's not even a keyhole."

"Open the door," commanded Maurice. "I want to go out."

"All right, all right," said William. "I'll open it."

At that moment Rose, who was still feeling and tapping about the walls, searching for secret springs and hollow sounds, bumped up against William in the semi-darkness. William, who was not expecting the bump, overbalanced against the door, at the same time letting go the edge by which he was holding it ajar. At that moment the door shut altogether, and the Seven were in darkness.

For a moment there was the dead silence of consternation. Maurice was the first to find his voice.

"Open the door," he wailed.

"Open the door, open the door!" shrieked the other little ones in tones of terror.

"Don't be an ass, William," shouted Charles. "Open the door!"

William was running his hands up and down the door frantically. He could just feel the crack where it fitted into the wall; but there was nothing—nothing—that he could take hold of—no crevice into which he could get his fingers.

"I can't," he gasped. "Charles, Charles, you come and try!"

Charles pushed his way to the frightened voice, and his hands met William's, and joined in their vain search.

"I can't feel anything," he said in a strained voice. "There's nothing here. Try down the crack. Have you a knife?"

"It wouldn't go in. If it did it would only break off. The door is so thick and heavy. Try the other side."

In the darkness they lost their bearings, and could feel nothing but the cold smooth surface of wall and door.

"Mummy, Mummy! Open the door. I want to go to Mummy!" shrieked Maurice at the top of his voice.

All the children joined in the clamor. Charles

and William began to kick at the door in a frenzy of fear, with wild shouts of "Daddy, Daddy!" For a few minutes the little room was a pandemonium of shrieking, struggling children. In the midst of the uproar Charles felt a tight clutch on his arm, and heard Rose's voice shouting in his ear.

"Charles, Charles!" she cried. "Tell them to stop. They'll hurt themselves. Where is Maurice?"

Charles could feel Rose trembling. He drew his hands across his eyes, and realized with a shock that tears were streaming down his cheeks. With a tremendous effort he straightened his back and pulled himself together. The thought of his mother crossed his mind. She had left him in charge—he was the eldest. He must do something to stop this din, and the struggling that was going on all round him.

"Rose, Rose, what are we to do?" he cried, in a hoarse voice that he hardly recognized as his own. He caught her hand in his, and with a gallant effort he added, "All right, all right. I'll tell William."

William was close by him, still kicking the door, and hammering at it with his hands. He took him by the shoulder and shook him as hard as he could.

"William, stop it a minute!" he shouted. "I want to speak to you."

William stopped hammering, and Charles heard him gasping for breath.

"William, old chap," he implored, "help me to see to the babies, and stop their crying."

"All right," said William, after a slight pause, and Charles felt a sudden great relief. He knew that William was going to be his usual, steady self again, and that with Rose, whose hand he was still tightly clasping, they could pacify the "babies." They began at once to call them by name, groping about in the darkness.

"It's all right," shouted Charles. "It's all right," shouted William and Rose. "Hullo, Stella, is that you? I know you by the parting in your hair. And here's Violet. Where's old Maurice?"

Gradually the cries of the younger ones grew quieter. Charles found Maurice lying on the floor. He picked him up in his arms, and then sat on the floor, holding him tight, and patting him with comforting vigor. Then he felt something wet and sticky on the fat, bare legs, and a new terror struck him. Had they in their first fright at being trapped and in darkness, knocked him down and trampled on him, and was this blood? His heart seemed to stop still at the thought. Maurice was such a jolly little beggar—and he, Charles, had been left in charge of him.

"Rose," he cried, "where are you? I'm afraid Maurice is hurt."

She groped her way to him, and felt Maurice gently all over. He was crying quietly now, and clutching Charles round the neck.

"I think he's all right," said Rose. "He's probably got a scratch or two; but if it was anything really bad that hurt him, he would cry much louder."

"You don't think he's getting weak, and going to die?" asked Charles anxiously.

"No, of course not. Why should he? He's so fat he just rolls about, and never comes to much harm. He's quite all right—aren't you, Maurice? I expect you're hungry."

Maurice sat up.

"I want my lunch," he said eagerly. "Mummy said we could have bananas."

Charles felt a great weight lifted from his heart.

"William," he cried. "How are you getting on?"

"Top-hole," answered his brother from the other side of the room. "I've got two."

This remark was followed by faint squeals and giggles. If it had not been dark Charles would have seen William sitting hunched up on the floor, with one arm round Stella, and the other round Anthony. He held them tight, and every now and then gave them a little squeeze—partly to assure himself that they were still there, and partly to cheer them up. Near by William were Rose and Violet, sitting close together, and occasionally comforting each other in whispers.

They sat thus for some time in silence broken now and then by a deep sobbing sigh from one or the other. Their cries and tears had been too violent to pass away quickly, and over these shuddering sighs they had no control.

"I'm very tired," said Rose at last.

"So am I, and my head's aching like anything," said William. "This place is terribly stuffy."

"Do you think that Daddy and Mummy have missed us yet?" asked Violet in a shaky voice.

"If they haven't they very soon will," said William. "If we shout and kick the door, don't you think they would hear us, if they were in the court-yard?"

"We might try it," agreed Charles. "It's no use sitting here and doing nothing. Let's take it in turns. You begin."

William got up and groped his way round the wall to the door, where he began to carry the plan into action with great vigor. At the noise he made fear again seized the younger children, and they began to shriek in unison.

"I say, William, it's no good," shouted Charles. "Daddy and Mummy are sure to look for us everywhere directly they miss us, and then they will be certain to find us in no time. You'll only start the babies off again, and we shall never be able to get them quiet. Besides, that door is so thick I don't really believe any sound could get through it."

"I don't either," said William, groping his way back again to his place to comfort his charges. "But we can't sit here and do nothing but think."

Maurice, having begun again, went on crying miserably, and Charles could not stop him.

"Look here," he said in desperation, "I'll tell you a story. We'll all take it in turns to tell one."

"A jolly good idea," said William; "but I hope we'll be found before it comes to my turn."

"Is Mummy coming soon?" wailed Maurice. "I want her."

"So do I!" sighed Violet, amid a fresh outburst of tears from the babies.

"I wish you wouldn't talk about her," said Charles.

"She'll come as soon as she can. Now, listen all, I'm going to tell you a story."

"What about?" they asked, cheering up a little.

"I don't know," confessed the worried Charles. "What would you like?"

"I want a story about the little frogs," said Maurice firmly.

"What little frogs?"

"You know, when they was naughty."

"Go on," said William, "make up anything. It's quite easy."

"Wait till it's your turn," protested Charles. "Then you won't think it so easy!"

Maurice gave a loud sob.

"Listen, listen," said Charles. "I'm just going to begin."

There was dead silence in the darkness of the little room, while the children hugged each other for comfort and waited.

THE STORY OF THE TWO FROGS

"Once upon a time," began Charles, "there were two little frogs."

"And their names were Jim and Jimmy," put in Maurice.

"No," said Charles firmly, feeling that he must

get away from family traditions, and launch out on a line of his own. "Their names were Bat and Batty."

"Jolly good names for them, too, I should think," put in William.

"Go on," commanded Maurice.

"They lived on the top of a stone in the middle of a river."

"Did they sleep there?" asked Maurice.

"People always sleep where they live," said Violet.

"No, they didn't sleep on top of the stone," continued Charles, emphatically. "The stone was hollow, and in the middle of it there was a tiny little hole that led into a big cave."

"Could they see in the little hole?" asked Maurice.

"Yes, they could, because these frogs could see in the dark."

"Lucky beggars!" remarked William.

"If you keep on interrupting me I shall never be able to tell you what they did," protested Charles. "So be quiet and listen."

"Go on," said Maurice; while William murmured, "Fire away, Charles."

"When the sun was shining they used to sit on top of the stone, and bathe in the river; but when it was wet they sat in their little cave."

"What did they eat?" inquired Maurice, who was feeling very hungry.

"They ate cakes and flies. In the summer, when it was hot, there were millions and millions of flies on the river, and every time that Bat and Batty bathed they caught five each."

"Did they catch them all in one mouthful?"

"No, they caught them one by one, and laid them out all in a row on the stone to dry."

"Did they bleed?" inquired Maurice anxiously.

"Yes, a lot. But it didn't hurt them much, because the frogs had practised till they could bite off heads very quickly. They bathed so often that they could get one hundred and ten in an hour. And when the flies were dried Bat and Batty took them down to the cave. In one corner of it they had a store-cupboard, full of sacks, where they kept their food for the winter."

"Did they make cakes?" asked Stella.

"Every day. And they always had them hot for tea."

"Where did they get the flour, and sugar, and eggs, and currants?"

"Close by the stone where Bat and Batty lived there was a mill. And every night, when the Miller was asleep, they used to go there and steal enough flour for the next day. They each had a little sack, made of rushes, which they filled to the brim. They got the flour first. Then they went out again to the Miller's kitchen, and got some sugar."

"How much sugar?" asked Maurice.

"They filled their sacks to the brim. They were very fond of sweet things, so they made their cakes half flour and half sugar."

"How ever did they get the eggs?" inquired Stella.

"On the banks of the river, about half a mile from their stone, was an ants' nest. And every night after they had got their flour and their sugar, and put it away in the sacks in their store-cupboard, they went to the ants' nest with their little rush baskets, and stole six eggs each."

"Twelve eggs in one cake," exclaimed Rose. "It must have been very rich."

"It was. And do you know what they used for currants?"

"The flies," shouted Anthony.

"You are quite right."

"How many did they put in one cake?" asked Stella.

"One hundred and ninety-three. They made it

every day directly after lunch, so that by tea time it was just done a lovely brown color."

"Did they have a stove?" asked Stella, ever practical.

"A lovely stove with an oven made exactly the right size for the cake. It was the newest pattern, with lots of patent things about it. You could take it all to pieces and put it together again quite easily, and at night it unfolded and made a lovely bed."

"Wasn't it very hard?" inquired Anthony.

"Not a bit. It had springs and a mattress inside, and after tea, when Bat and Batty went to bed, it was still warm, so it was a good bed to have in the winter. In the summer, they had hammocks that they carried up on top of the stone, and they slept out of doors."

"How lovely!" everyone cried.

"And one day the Miller looked at his flour and his sugar, and he thought it was going very fast. He guessed it was some little mice who had stolen it, and he was very cross with his cat for letting them take it."

"But it wasn't mice!" crowed Maurice.

"Of course it wasn't. It was Bat and Batty. But the Miller never guessed that."

"I did!" said Maurice proudly.

"He was a silly Miller. So he got a little mouse-trap, with a little piece of cheese in it, and put it down all ready to catch a mouse. Then he went to bed. And when Bat and Batty came for the flour they saw the little trap.

" 'What a beautiful thing!' said Bat. 'It would just do for a rack to fasten up over our stove, to warm the plates to put our cake on.'

" 'So it would,' said Batty. 'If we hurry up we shall have plenty of time to take it home, and come back again for our flour and sugar.'

" 'We will have a good look at it first,' said Bat. 'What do you think that little wire hook is for?'

"They had learnt a lot at school about algebra and arithmetic and carpentry, and they were always top at their lessons—like William and me."

"Ha ha!" ejaculated William. "Clever chaps!"

"So they walked round the mousetrap and ex-amined it very carefully, and then they both saw the trick of it.

" 'We must both stand on the top of the cage,' they said, 'and pull back the wire hook. Then the door will drop down. I wonder what it's for!'

"They did this very carefully, and then took the mousetrap home. And that night, after they had got their flour and sugar and eggs, they fixed it up over their stove as a rack, and so had hot plates to put their cakes on for ever after."

"Jolly good idea," said William. "Wasn't it a good idea, Maurice?"

"Hush!" said Charles. "He's fast asleep."

"I think Stella and Anthony have gone off, too," said William. "Go on with your story, Charles."

"That's the end. Now it is your turn."

"I'll tell you about Ulysses and the Cyclops," said William, yawning. "I feel awfully sleepy."

"So do I," said Charles. "I don't think there's much air in here. Fire away with Ulysses."

CHAPTER IV

THE SEVEN FOUND

MR. and Mrs. Bailey looked at each other anxiously when no answer came to their calls, and no children came running up.

"Perhaps they are hiding from us for fun," suggested Mr. Bailey.

"They wouldn't hide for long, when they know it's lunch-time," said his wife.

"I suppose not. They must have wandered away somewhere."

Mrs. Bailey turned pale. "Quick, Arthur," she said. "Go to the top of the wall and look outside. Perhaps they climbed over."

Mr. Bailey was on the wall before she had finished speaking, anxiously scanning the surrounding rocks and the shore.

"I can see two or three carts coming piled up with furniture. That's a good thing. But the children are not in sight."

"Where can they be, Arthur?"

"Perhaps they saw Robert or Matilda, and went inside with them. Robert! Robert! Matilda!" shouted Mr. Bailey.

He ran back to the door and met Robert coming out in answer to his call.

"Have you seen the children? Where are they? We left them playing out here."

Robert shook his head.

"We were having a bit of bread and cheese in the kitchen," he said. "They haven't been in there."

"Then where can they be? They must be somewhere; but I can't find them."

Robert shook his head again.

"It's a terrible lonely place," he said mournfully, "and full of danger to children. I'll see if they are indoors."

Robert disappeared for a couple of minutes and then returned, shaking his head. "There's a crier up in the town. We better tell him and he can go round announcing the loss. If you offered a bit of a reward you may get them back, but——"

"Nonsense!" interrupted Mr. Bailey sharply, "they can't have gone far. I want you to come and help me find them. You know this place better than we do."

"Do you think they're inside or out?" asked Robert. "If they are outside I'll go up to the lookout, and if they've not strayed too far give them a shout."

"I don't know where they are, but I left them playing in the courtyard, and I didn't hear them come inside again."

Matilda joined them, and they set out, under the direction of Mr. Bailey, to search the place, systematically—looking for the children very much as, nearly two hours earlier, the children had looked for enemies and robbers.

"They can't be here," said Mrs. Bailey at last, "or we should have seen or heard something of them long before now. They must have gone exploring outside the walls."

"They're not usually so disobedient," said their father. "I shall give the boys a good caning. Perhaps they went to meet the furniture, and got off the track to paddle, or collect shells."

He set off at a run down the causeway, followed closely by Mrs. Bailey, with Robert and Matilda bringing up the rear. At the end of it the men with the furniture were just beginning to unload their carts.

"Hi!" shouted Mr. Bailey when he was within hailing distance. "Have you seen any children about?"

"Children! Where?" asked the man in charge. "Not anywhere down this way. Wait a minute though, now I come to think of it, I did see one at the farm."

"Ah, very likely they are there," said Mr. Bailey, seizing on the faint hope. "I will go and see."

He was off at once, leaving his wife standing by the furniture.

"What children do you want?" asked the man. "Have you lost any?"

"Yes, *seven*," said Mrs. Bailey, halfway between a laugh and a sob.

"You've lost seven children!" cried the man. He seemed amazed at such carelessness.

"Yes," said Robert, who had come up looking more doleful than ever. "I never heard tell of *seven* being lost before, but there was one lost five years ago come August. Just about here it was, too."

"And where did they find it?" inquired Mrs. Bailey eagerly.

"The body was washed up a week later, somewhere round the other side of the island," said Robert, while the man in charge of the furniture shook his head vigorously at him, as a signal that he disapproved of such tactless talk.

Mrs. Bailey's heart seemed to her to stop beating altogether for a moment. Then she turned away very quickly and ran to meet her husband, who was returning alone from the farm.

"No sign of them," he cried. Then he saw her look of distress. "Now don't get frightened, Alice. They are sure to be safe somewhere. Let's sit down a moment and think. What would they be most likely to do when we left them?"

"I don't think they would get over the wall, when we had told them to play about inside and not go far away, especially as the boys were in charge of the younger ones."

"No, I don't think they would," agreed Mr. Bailey. "So we will go back and make a thorough search of the Fort, and the whole place inside the walls. They may have got locked into one of the rooms, or have come across something so interesting that they have forgotten the time."

They jumped up from the grass where they were sitting, and ran back toward the Fort to continue their search.

"Shall we bring the furniture along now?" asked the foreman, as they came up to him.

"Yes," said Mr. Bailey, "and I'll be with you directly we've found the children. Dump it down in the courtyard."

With Robert and Matilda they went into every room in the Fort. They shouted till their voices grew tired and hoarse, the sound of the children's names went traveling down the long corridors, and echoing back in solemn mockery. But of answering cries there were none, and though Mr. Bailey stooped down many times with his ear to the ground he heard no sound.

"Hark!" said Mrs. Bailey once. "Wasn't that a child's cry?"

"Only a seagull," answered Robert. "They're terribly alike—a seagull's cry and a baby's. Not much to choose between them I say."

Then they went into the courtyard; but still there was no sign of the Seven.

By this time the men had unloaded the van, and

brought up the furniture, which they had piled all together, and they now joined the distracted little group of searchers.

"Oh, Arthur, what shall we do?" exclaimed Mrs. Bailey, becoming more and more frightened.

"My father used to be stationed out here with his regiment," said one of the men, "and I've often been over it with him, and know every inch of the place. Have you looked in the guard-rooms, and the cellars?"

"Yes, we have," said Robert.

"Oh, please look again," implored Mrs. Bailey, clutching at any straw of help. "Perhaps we have missed them somewhere."

Again they went the round of the Fort; but with no success.

"What about the old storeroom, Robert?" suggested the man. "Could they have got in there?"

"That's all overgrown now, and hasn't been used for years," said Robert. "But we'd best look there before we give up all hope."

He led them to the door which Stella had spied with such excitement earlier in the day. He thrust aside the bushes that grew in front, and put his shoulder against it.

He gave one big push, and the door swung open before him. The afternoon sunshine flooded the little room, and a strange sight met the eyes of the group of searchers crowding round, and for a moment struck them silent.

There were the children, huddled up on the floor, still and silent. With one glance round, their father and mother saw that all seven were there: Charles, sitting with his back against the wall, and Maurice in his arms; William, his head sunk on his knees, and Anthony and Stella on either side leaning against him; and Rose and Violet lying close together in the corner.

"Oh, Arthur! are they alive?" said Mrs. Bailey, and with a sobbing cry she was in the little room, kneeling down by the children, and calling them by name.

One by one they opened their eyes and looked round in a dazed way. Maurice, feeling his mother's arms round his, clutched her tightly and began to whimper. The others stirred uneasily, and William lifted his head from his knees and muttered in a far-away voice.

"And in the cave," he said, "the Cyclops kept his sheep——"

"Wake up, William," said his father sharply, not knowing that he had fallen asleep in the middle of a story.

Very gently he shook both boys, and helped them to their feet.

"We had better get them all outside into the fresh air," he said. "They are half-dazed, and no wonder!"

"Are the babies all right?" mumbled Charles. "It was all my fault in the beginning when we trod on them."

"It was mine just as much as his," put in William.

"Everybody is all right now," said Mr. Bailey soothingly, thinking the boys were still half-asleep, and wandering in their dreams.

"It must have been pretty stuffy in there and no mistake," remarked the foreman, who had been examining the little room. "There's no ventilation. A good thing that the room is no smaller, and we found them when we did. Once in, with the door shut, there's nobody who could get out again. A regular death trap I call it!"

"Bed's the place for those children," said another of the men, who was the father of a large family of his own. "They're worn out."

"You're right," agreed the foreman heartily. "Shall we get the beds up, ma'am?"

"Oh, yes, please," said Mrs. Bailey gratefully. "Do they want airing?"

"Everything is as dry as a bone," said her husband, "it hasn't rained since we left London. I'll go and see to things while you stay here with the children."

He went off with Robert and the other men, and Mrs. Bailey and Matilda were left to comfort the pathetic-looking little group that sat bunched up on the grass around them. Now that Mrs. Bailey had time to have a good look at the children in the light of day, the thought of the plight in which they had been came upon her in full force, and tears ran down her face as she murmured little endearing names and broken phrases.

The elder ones began to hobble about, stretching and rubbing their cramped limbs; the little ones lay on the grass just as they had been put down. The faces of all seven were grimed with dirt, their legs and hands were scratched and bleeding, and their clothes were dusty and torn.

"They want a wash," said Matilda.

Her matter-of-fact voice and words recalled Mrs. Bailey to the need of action.

"Those are words of wisdom," she said. "When I can see your faces again I shall perhaps realize that I have really found you. Matilda, have you any hot water?"

"Yes, the kettle is boiling. And there is some chicken broth ready."

"How splendid of you!" cried Mrs. Bailey, feeling a wave of gratitude to the stolid woman standing at her side.

By the time that Mr. Bailey rejoined them, the children were transformed beings, all sitting, scrubbed and combed, and dressed in their pyjamas, round Matilda's kitchen table, drinking chicken broth out of mugs.

"What a jolly family party!" he exclaimed, beaming with smiles, a great gratitude in his heart at seeing them all alive and happy.

"I've got Tim's mug," cried Anthony joyously.

"Who's Tim?"

"Matilda's little boy. He's a sailor. Can I be a sailor when I'm a man?"

"Certainly, you may. You can be anything you like—if your mother approves."

"Oh, Arthur," said Mrs. Bailey, "I'm so happy! I approve of anything and everything."

"Then there are seven beds put up, and ready for your approval," announced her husband.

"Matilda and I'll go and make them at once, while the children finish their meal. I am beginning to feel hungry myself," said Mrs. Bailey. "Matilda is going to make us an omelet directly we have settled the children."

"What a treat!" cried Mr. Bailey. "I feel still hungrier. We had better pass on our picnic basket to the furniture men. We wasted a lot of their time, and they have worked like Trojans."

"A good idea," agreed his wife, as she and Matilda hurried away to prepare the beds.

"I've got grease all over my legs, Daddy," announced Maurice proudly, thinking it quite time he got a little attention.

"Lucky boy!" said his father, knowing that all healing ointments went by the name of "grease," and that it was considered a mark of high distinction to have a scratch bad enough to need their aid.

"I have got grease on mine, too," said Anthony, not to be outdone; and Mr. Bailey had to make a round of the table to view all the scratches and bruises, exhibited with happy pride.

"Well!" he exclaimed, "you are a lot of wounded

warriors!   Tomorrow you must tell me the whole story of how you got such scars.   But now go on with your meal, so that you will be ready to tumble into your beds when they're made."

"Aren't we going to have our lunch?" asked Anthony, and a clamor at once arose as they all took up the cry.

"Lunch!" exclaimed Mr. Bailey. "When you have had that lovely chicken broth!"

"That's only a drink," said Charles.

"We don't count it as anything," agreed William.

"I want a banana," protested Maurice.

"Splendid!" cried Mr. Bailey. "There's nothing much wrong with you anyhow. But here comes your mother—and now to bed! And when you wake up you shall all have as much to eat as you want. That's a promise."

Rose

CHAPTER V

THE FIRST PICNIC

"WHAT a glorious day!" exclaimed Mr. Bailey, for the hundredth time, after breakfast the next morning. "I see that the glass is falling, so I think we should be wise to take advantage of such wonderful sunny weather while it lasts, and do a little exploring of the island."

"Oh, Arthur!" expostulated his wife. "We have so much unpacking to do, and there are those pegs

to be put up in the bedrooms, and the pictures to be
hung, and endless other things to set straight.
Everything is so jumbled together that I can't find
a thing."

Mr. Bailey hesitated.

"Don't you think we might take a day or two off?"
he asked wistfully. "We have plenty of time before
us in which to get straight."

His wife could never withstand his wishes for long,
and she knew from past experience of holidays that
he would never settle down happily till his passion
for exact topographical knowledge was satisfied.
She made a little grimace at him, and laughed.

"Do you want to make a day of it, and have a
picnic?" she asked.

He beamed assent, and the Seven shouted with delight. She could resist no longer. With Matilda's
help, lunch was packed into three large knapsacks
and a basket, and soon they were filing along the
causeway. Mr. Bailey led the way, with a knapsack
on his back, a basket in one hand and a large stick in
the other. Next came Charles and William, each
with a knapsack, followed by Mrs. Bailey and the
rest of the Seven, all jumping about with excitement,
and none of them any the worse for their adventure
in the dark storeroom.

"Where shall we go?" asked Mr. Bailey, waiting for them all to come up with him.

"The bay that we came along yesterday looked very attractive," said his wife.

"Yes, but we've seen that, and I think we should explore in the other direction," said Mr. Bailey, firmly. "Just look at the map for a moment."

He dumped down his basket, and spread out his beloved map of the island.

"Now if we go up the valley in front of us, on our left, we shall strike this footpath on the top. We follow it round the cliffs for half a mile, and then drop down into this bay, which is marked as sandy. Then we can bathe, and have our lunch, and paddle about, and be back in time for tea."

"Don't you think it rather far for the babies?" objected his wife, doubtfully.

"Not a bit of it," cried Mr. Bailey. "They are all very good walkers. And coming home my basket will be empty, and I can give them rides on my shoulder in turns."

"Can I have a ride now?" asked Maurice.

"No, certainly not, young lazybones. Come along, let us be going. Follow me."

He set out along the valley path. The journey up took a long time, because the children discovered some blackberries on low bushes growing on the steep sides of the hill.

"Blackberries in July!" exclaimed Mr. Bailey. "That shows how sheltered and sunny it is here. *What* a glorious place!"

> "Blackberries, blackberries, ripe in July
> On the beautiful island of Alder*nye*—
> Let's have a feast,
> I will, at least,
> While the cows graze and the sun's in the sky,"

sang William, at the top of his voice.

"Ha, ha!" laughed his father. "William in poetic mood again. Can't you give us another verse?"

"I could," said William, "but it's your turn now."

"Then here goes," said his father, not to be outdone:

> "So they all had a feast on that beautiful shore,
> Till they lay on the ground and could swallow no more;
> 'Twas writ on their tombstones:
> 'Just here lie the dry bones
> Of those who died feasting on blackberries galore.' "

"What a gloomy idea to have in such a lovely spot!" said Mrs. Bailey. "Don't you think we might settle down and have our picnic here?"

"No, no," said Mr. Bailey, quickly. "There's a much better place farther on, and we must have a bathe. Come along, let us mount upwards. Maurice, take hold the end of my stick, and I'll pull you."

Very soon they got to the top of the valley side, and found themselves on a wild stretch of heather and gorse, intersected by grassy paths and rabbit tracks.

"What a delicious smell!" exclaimed Mrs. Bailey. "The paths are just beds of wild flowers."

"And what a view!" said her husband, gazing out to sea. "Just look at those rocky islands. We must explore them some day. We shall probably find some wonderful bathing pools there. But today we must make for our sandy bay."

They sauntered slowly along, kept moving in the right direction by constant calls and reminders from Mr. Bailey.

"What is that cottage on the edge of the cliff?" asked Mrs. Bailey. "It looks quite deserted."

"An old telegraph station," answered her husband. "It's marked on the map. We'll go and have a look at it."

The Seven rushed on in front, and were soon looking into it through the windows.

"What a pity the door's locked," said Charles. "Shall we smash a window and climb into it?"

"Oh, Charles!" exclaimed his mother. "How can you think of such a thing after your experience of yesterday?"

"This is different," said Charles, "it's quite light inside."

"Look at that rusty iron rope hanging over the cliff," said William. "Do you think I could climb down by it?"

"Boys," said Mrs. Bailey firmly, "you are to keep with us, and you are not to do anything, nor go anywhere, by yourselves, unless I say you may."

"Oh, dear!" cried William. "But suppose Father tells us to?"

"He won't!" said Mr. Bailey. "Today we're exploring. When we know the island we can potter round looking for further adventures. One thing at a time. And here is the path down the cliffs to the shore."

"What a dangerous place!" exclaimed Mrs. Bailey, looking timidly over the edge. "We can't possibly get down there. It looks like a path for goats."

"It's quite all right, I'm sure," said her husband. "It's marked on the map as a way down to the shore. The boys and I will go on ahead to see that it's all right and then I'll come back for you and the children."

"Can't I come too?" asked Rose pleadingly.

"Yes, but no more of you. I'll go first, and you

follow. Look where you place your feet, and make certain the ground is firm before each step you take."

They disappeared over the edge of the cliff, and Mrs. Bailey and the four younger children began to pick the wildflowers that grew all around them. She was just beginning to feel worried about the rest of her family when Mr. Bailey's head reappeared over the cliff, toward which she was casting many anxious glances.

"The path is quite good, though a little narrow in parts," he said. "I've left Rose and the boys at the bottom, with the lunch. Come along, all of you. I'll take charge of Maurice."

Very slowly they wended their way down the narrow zigzag path, Mr. Bailey holding Maurice firmly by the belt and issuing instructions to the others, and Mrs. Bailey uttering faint protests at the most precipitous places. Happily none of the children felt any fear, and giddiness was unknown to them. The only danger lay in their inexperience and consequent lack of all caution.

At last they reached the shore in safety, and were welcomed by the older ones, who had watched their descent with great interest.

"What a time you took to come down!" exclaimed Charles. "I ran all the way."

"I think it was very sporting of the babies to come at all," said Rose, loyally. "May we bathe now?"

"You may," said Mr. Bailey. He knew from experience that there would be no peace till that was over.

"That was something like a bathe!" cried Rose when they had been ordered back to shore with much firmness by Mr. Bailey, and were dressing in the sunshine.

"What is there for lunch?" asked William.

"That's just what I was wondering," said his father. "Let's all have a race to that blue rock, and then I think it will be time to unpack the knapsacks."

Mr. Bailey won the race, and they all gathered round for the crowning delight of every picnic, fresh and glowing from their exercise.

"This flat rock is made for a table," said Mrs. Bailey. "Now, children, sit round in a semicircle, and we'll spread our lunch on it."

The rock table soon presented the appearance of a festive board. There were piles and piles of sandwiches, two large mince pies and a jam tart, ten hard-boiled eggs—"Two for you, Arthur," said

Mrs. Bailey, laughing—nine rock cakes, and nine bananas.

"No wonder our loads were so heavy, boys," said Mr. Bailey. "What a feast!"

"There's nothing to drink," said his wife, "so you must none of you say you are thirsty."

"If you do you'll be sent home to bed," threatened Mr. Bailey, with a smile that took all the sting from his threat.

For some time there was silence. Mrs. Bailey was the first to break it.

"When will it be high tide, Arthur?" she asked.

"At six o'clock," said her husband, "and then there'll be no sand here, and the sea will be dashing against the rocks."

Mrs. Bailey shivered. "We shall be home long before then, I hope," she said.

"Of course we shall be; but before we go we shall see it come dashing in over those rocks. It must be a fine sight in a storm. Have you children finished your lunch?"

"Is there anything more to eat?" asked William.

"No," said Mr. Bailey. "My question was merely a polite way of declaring the meal at an end. We have finished everything. Now you can all go and paddle, while your mother and I have a little rest. Be óff, but don't go far. I'll be with you in half an hour."

The Seven scampered away, and Mr. Bailey settled himself comfortably with his hat over his eyes and his pipe in his mouth, while Mrs. Bailey leaned restfully against a rock.

Half an hour later she woke with a start, out of a dream in which she heard a voice calling urgently to her. The voice continued to call, and when she opened her eyes she saw Charles, flushed and panting, standing before her.

"Mummy, mummy!" he gasped. "William has climbed up and can't climb down."

"Arthur!" she shouted, shaking her husband. "Wake up! Something has happened!"

In one second Mr. Bailey was wide awake, in the next he was sprinting along the sands by Charles' side. There were no children in sight.

"Where are they?" he cried.

"The other side of those rocks," panted Charles, who could hardly keep up the pace.

'And there, surely enough, Mr. Bailey saw them, as he rounded the corner. They stood in a group, all heads lifted, gazing up at the cliffs. His glance followed theirs, and then, about thirty feet up the face of the rocks, which at this point rose almost perpendicularly, he saw a small figure that he knew to be William. Hanging down the rock from the top to within a few feet of the ground was the rusty iron rope they had spied from above. William had evidently swarmed up this rope, and was now clutching on to it, his feet resting on a narrow ledge, formed by a fissure that ran across the rock. Above and below this ledge it was sheer, with no foothold anywhere to be seen on its smooth surface.

"He stood on my shoulder and climbed up, till he could reach the rope," gasped Charles, "and now I don't think he can go any farther."

"Oh, Daddy!" cried Rose, turning a pale face and horrified eyes to her father. "I'm glad you're here."

"What shall we do, Arthur?" exclaimed Mrs. Bailey, who had just come running up. "Can you climb the rope? Shall I go for help?"

"If I climb the rope," said Mr. Bailey, who had been examining the cliffs and considering plans of rescue, "I shall shake it, and William will almost certainly lose his hold and fall. And I can't climb to him in any other way; there's no foothold that would serve a goat. I think he's tired out. He probably saw the ledge and stopped for a breather, and now, seeing the drop below him and the height above, he has lost his nerve and is afraid to move, either up or down."

"What shall we do? Oh, what shall we do?" cried Mrs. Bailey in a voice that she tried in vain to keep steady.

"I must go and get a rope and assistance, and come down the cliffs to him from above," said her husband. "I shall have to go to the Fort, and at the very least it will be half an hour before I can be back. You stay here. He has a good foothold, and if he keeps his head he'll be all right."

He gave a last glance up at the figure that looked so small against the vast wall of rock and, putting his hands to his mouth trumpetwise, he shouted:

"Stay—where—you—are—William. I—am—going—to—get—a—rope. Don't—move. I—wont—be—long."

He saw William nod his head two or three times. Then he turned, and ran at full speed for the cliff path.

Mrs. Bailey, with the children clustering round her, stood at the foot of the rock. She glanced at the watch on her wrist. It was five minutes to three.

Her husband had said half an hour, and that, she knew, would be a record time in which to do the journey to the Fort and back to the top of the cliffs. Then he might be delayed by a dozen or so mishaps: he might not find any rope handy; Robert might be gone into the town; even when he returned there might be no tree or post above to which he could fasten a rope. All these possibilities, and many more, rushed through her mind.

"Charles," she said, "I think you had better go up the path to the top of the cliffs, and stand on a spot exactly above William. Then your father won't have to waste any time in looking for it, when he comes back with the rope."

"Yes, I'll go at once," answered Charles, only too glad at the prospect of doing something to help, and preparing to be off.

"Slip on your shoes first," said his mother. "When I see you at the top I'll walk a few paces to right or left, according to your position, and when I stand still you will know that you're directly over the spot where he is. I won't make any other signs to you, or William may think I am signaling to him, and try to move."

"Yes, I understand. And I may be able to help

with the rope when Daddy comes," said Charles. He looked very white and drawn, and Mrs. Bailey knew what he was suffering. William was so near to him in age, and from their earliest days they had been inseparable companions, often teasing and scrapping with each other, but never happy apart.

He ran off, and soon disappeared round the rocks. Mrs. Bailey looked at her watch again. It was three o'clock.

She could never remember afterward how she spent the next half hour, but she always said it brought her first gray hairs. William remained absolutely still and she felt that she herself must also remain still in sympathy with him. Only once, when Charles appeared on the edge of the cliff above, did she shift her position a pace or two. The other children stood round, silent for once as they realized the danger that lurked so near.

She could never have told how many times she looked at her watch, and counted the slow seconds as they passed by. But at last the hands marked the half hour, and she felt her knees trembling under her, as dreadful thoughts of accidents that might have overtaken her husband and delayed him chased one another across her mind.

At last the hands marked the half hour.

Then suddenly she saw him by Charles' side on the cliff. Another figure stood by him. That must be Robert, she thought. In his hand was a coil of rope, which he was busy fastening to the stake from which hung the iron one, and as she looked she saw him throw the coil far out in the air. It spun along, like a snake about to strike, and then fell down the face of the rock, only a few yards from William. The next moment she saw her husband climbing down it, hand over hand, with a second rope about his waist.

She knew that he was not in training for such a feat as he was embarked upon, and now she held her breath with fear for him. Yet she also knew his powers of endurance, his set purpose, and his cool head in any emergency. And as she watched him, as he let himself steadily down, all her confidence in him surged uppermost, though her heart was beating so hard that the noise of it rang in her ears.

Maurice began to sob, but no one took any notice of him, so intent were they on the scene being enacted above. Nearer and nearer came Mr. Bailey to the small still figure. Then, at last, he was within a few yards of William, they saw him stop, they saw his foot stretched out, feeling for a foothold on the ledge. He had found it. He was edging his way along the rock to William. He was touching him. A sigh of relief went up from the watchers, and the children's silence was broken.

"What's he going to do now?" gasped Rose.

"Will he climb down?"

"Will he carry William?"

"Be quiet, children," said Mrs. Bailey. "I think he is tying a rope round him."

They saw him stooping over William, one hand still holding his own rope, the other busily engaged with the second rope he had slung round him. He put this round the boy, and they saw him adjusting it under his arms. Then both figures were still. Mr. Bailey seemed to be talking, and they saw him rubbing William's arms and legs. A few moments later the rope was drawn tight from above in response to a signal from Mr. Bailey, and very slowly William began to move upward. He still held the iron rope, and they had seen his father place his hands a little higher on it, evidently telling him to help himself upward by its aid. But when his feet were about level with Mr. Bailey's, the boy let go his hold on it, and hung suspended by the waist. Would the rope hold his whole weight? Would Robert and Charles be able to haul him up? Then up, up he went, little by little. He was within a few yards of the top. They saw a hand stretched out to him. The next minute he disappeared over the top.

Mrs. Bailey sat down on the sand, tears streaming down her face, a great thanksgiving in her heart. In those last minutes of strained watching she had thought only of William, and the sudden relief of his rescue almost overcame her. But the next moment she remembered that her husband now stood in William's place. He had remained there quite still while the boy was drawn up; now he was looking about him, evidently considering his next move. He seemed to come to a decision. He swung himself round facing the rock; then started to continue his way down, hand over hand. Slowly and carefully he came, and Mrs. Bailey guessed that he was very tired, and as he came nearer she could hear his gasping breaths. He was at the end of the rope; he dropped on to the rocks below, and lay there with closed eyes.

Mrs. Bailey knelt down beside him.

"Oh, Arthur, Arthur," was all she could say, and she said it over and over again. His face was scratched and grazed, his hands were torn and bleeding, and his clothes hung in great rents.

He opened his eyes and smiled. "I shall be all

right in a minute or two," he said. "I'm not used to that sort of thing—not in proper training."

"Mummy," said Rose suddenly, "the tide is coming up very fast. I think we shall have to hurry, or we shan't be able to get round the rocks, to our cliff path."

Mr. Bailey jumped to his feet and took one look round.

"Come quickly, all of you," he shouted. "Run. Or we shall be cut off by the tide, and I don't feel that I can stand any more excitement today!"

CHAPTER VI

THE PLEASURES OF RABBITING

"IS William all right?" panted Mrs. Bailey, when they had rounded the rocks and arrived, sea-splashed but triumphant, at the foot of the cliff path, where they had left their shoes and stockings and picnic things.

"He seemed dazed," said her husband. "When I got down to him he was clinging so tightly to the rope that I had great difficulty in getting him to unclasp his hands. He was numb, but after I had given him a rub he came round a bit."

"Poor boy," murmured his mother.

They put on their shoes and collected their things, and began slowly to climb up the cliff path. The children were very quiet and subdued and, picking their steps carefully, got to the top without mishap. Mrs. Bailey led the way, her thoughts bent on getting to William.

"They are still there," she called back to her husband. "I'll go on."

She broke into a run, and quickly joined Robert and the two boys. William was sitting on the grass, a sorry figure, still looking pale and dazed, and Charles stood by him, giving him an occasional pat on the shoulder. Robert was untying his rope from the old iron post.

"This is a terrible place for boys," he said. "You never know from one minute to another whether it won't be their last."

"Oh, William," cried Mrs. Bailey, "what a fright you gave us! Get up now, and come along home. I'm dying for a cup of tea."

She helped the bruised and bleeding boy to his feet.

"I shall make you all suits of corduroy," she said. "Ordinary suits are hopeless. I shall never be able to mend that one. It would hardly be of any use to a scarecrow. And your father's is not much better."

The rest of the family had now arrived, and all the children gazed at William in silent sympathy.

"Let's be getting home," said Mr. Bailey. "I want my tea."

He took William by the arm and, followed by the rest of the family, wended his way along the cliff and down the valley homeward.

"Have you any grease, Mummy?" asked Maurice solemnly, after a long silence.

"I have plenty at home, Maurice. Do you want any?"

"He always says yes if you offer him grease," remarked Rose.

"No, I don't," said Maurice indignantly. "I want Daddy to have some. He's all bleedin'. And I want William to have some. He's all bleedin' too."

"Now that's very kind of you, Maurice," said Mr. Bailey, looking back over his shoulder. "I am sure we shall want a whole pot of grease to soothe all the scratches we have. I think I shall have a day in bed tomorrow. And William, I am sure, will keep me company."

"Oh, Daddy," cried Charles, "we are going out rabbiting tomorrow."

"That's news to me. Are you taking your guns?" asked his father, with a twinkle in his eye.

"We are going with Robert," answered Charles very seriously, evidently feeling that the subject was not one to joke about. "We only decided to go when we were waiting for you on the cliff. He is going to show us how to catch them."

"Yes, and skin 'em too," said Robert, who had followed them with his rope and was now walking along at their side.

"Isn't that rather cruel?" asked Mrs. Bailey, looking at her husband.

"It certainly sounds cruel," he said.

"Oh, no, Daddy. The place is overrun with them. Robert says so. They eat everything in people's gardens."

"I suppose they do," said Mrs. Bailey. "But I do hope that catching them is not a very cruel business."

"It's got to be done," said Robert. "The way I catch 'em is very neat and painless and doesn't spoil the rabbit for cooking the same as shooting 'em mostly does."

"If we have to kill in this world—and it certainly does seem to be necessary—it's a good thing to learn to do it in the neatest and quickest way possible, as Robert says," declared Mr. Bailey. "And if ever the boys should become explorers, or pioneers in some new land, the knowledge of how to trap animals for food may one day save their lives."

"Yes, I suppose you are right, Arthur," agreed his wife loyally, though a little doubtfully.

They reached the end of the path through the valley, and were soon walking along the causeway. Matilda met them at the courtyard door.

"The water is ready for hot baths," she announced, gazing fixedly at Mr. Bailey and William, who certainly looked as if they needed them. "Tea will be ready when you are."

"Come on, William old chap," said his father. "I see we are for it. We will be ready for tea in ten minutes, Matilda," and with his arm still through the boy's he disappeared down the corridor to the bathroom.

"I think we shall all be better for a wash and a change," said Mrs. Bailey. "Come along, children. Tea in ten minutes, please, Matilda."

And punctually ten minutes later Mrs. Bailey was seated at the long dining-table, launching the younger members of the family on the meal, so that she might have more leisure for pouring out tea when her husband and William should arrive.

In a very short time Mr. Bailey came in, looking very fresh, clad in a gorgeous flowered dressing-gown that the children greatly admired.

"I have bound up William's hands and packed him off to bed," he said. "The boy is completely done up. He has not uttered a word since he was hauled up the cliff. I have promised to send Charles to him with a good tea."

"I'll go and get a tray, and take it now," said Charles, jumping up from his seat at the table. "I expect he's jolly hungry."

He got the tray and Mrs. Bailey loaded it with a tempting-looking array. Matilda had made them hot buttered toast and a dough cake, and there were, besides, a dish of lettuces, some homemade strawberry jam, some honey, several plates of bread and butter and a large jug of milk.

"There," she said, "I have given him a little of everything. And here is the bell. Tell him to ring it if he wants any more."

"Better tell him that he need not eat all that is on the tray if he doesn't want to," said Mr. Bailey.

"Oh, Arthur," expostulated his wife. "After such an afternoon the poor boy will be hungry."

"If he feels anything like me he will be *very* hungry," agreed Mr. Bailey. "But you must admit that such a quantity of food, all collected together in so small a space, does look rather alarming."

Charles staggered off with the tray, but in a few moments he came staggering back again.

"William is fast asleep," he said somewhat breathlessly. "Shall I wake him up?"

"Certainly not," said his father. "Sleep will do him more good than anything else."

"He shall have whatever he likes for tea when he wakes," said Mrs. Bailey.

But William was still sleeping soundly that night when they went to bed; he was still sleeping soundly when Mrs. Bailey crept in to look at him in the middle of the night; and it was only when Charles jumped out of bed the next morning that he stirred and opened his eyes.

"Is it tea-time yet?" he asked sleepily.

"Tea-time? Why, it's nearly breakfast-time," cried Charles. "Can't you smell the bacon frying?"

William came down to breakfast, to all appearances quite recovered from his climbing adventure. He still had his hands swathed in bandages, and Charles had helped him to dress. Charles had also washed his brother's face and combed his hair, and it was evident that he had spared no energy in doing so.

"I have never seen your face so shiningly clean, or your hair so well brushed and plastered down," said Mr. Bailey. "I think I shall make it a rule in future that you two boys perform this part of your toilet for each other."

The boys laughed.

"He put soap in my eyes, and my head is sore—he brushed it so hard," complained William.

"I didn't," declared Charles. "It took me ages, and he never said thank you, but grumbled all the time."

"You must have your hands seen to directly after breakfast, William," interposed Mr. Bailey. "I think it will be some time before you can leave off the bandages."

"Yes," said Mrs. Bailey, "we shall have to see that the cuts are healed first, or you will get dirt in them and probably poison them. It would be a good idea, I think, to put on a large pair of gloves over the bandages."

"Have you a pair to lend him, dear?" asked Mr. Bailey sweetly.

"Well, I was thinking of a pair of yours, Arthur," said his wife.

"Ah, I thought as much! My best wash-leather ones, I suppose?"

"Well, Arthur, it *is* most important to keep the bandages firm."

"May we go rabbiting?" asked William eagerly. "Robert wants to start early."

"Oh, certainly," said his father. "In my best wash-leather gloves you will be quite all right."

"Oh, Arthur!" exclaimed his wife. "Do you really mind lending them?"

"Not at all," said Mr. Bailey. "But don't use the word 'lending,' because you know that by the time William has been out rabbiting with them, and worn them for a few days, there won't be anything left of them."

Mrs. Bailey jumped up from the table, and came round and kissed him. "I will give you a new pair for Christmas," she promised cheerfully.

Her husband groaned. "From the moment that you first mentioned gloves I knew that mine were doomed. I'll go and get them."

"Can't I go rabbiting, too?" asked Rose.

"And I?—and I?—and me too?" shouted the younger ones in chorus.

"Robert says that he can take only William and me," replied Charles. "He says a crowd would frighten all the rabbits into the sea."

"I tell you what," said Mr. Bailey. "We'll let those two bad boys go off with Robert, and when they are safely out of the way, we'll go fishing."

"How lovely!" cried Rose, and the younger ones shouted with glee.

"You might wait till tomorrow," complained Charles, "and then we could come too."

"My dear Charles," said his father, "you go off and leave us to our own devices; do you expect us to sit quite still all day, waiting for your return? No, no."

"Then may we all go fishing again tomorrow?"

"Well," answered Mr. Bailey musingly, "I had thought of hiring Mr. James' boat tomorrow, and going with your mother to explore the island on the other side of the channel—the Swinge as it's called. I hear that the tide will be just right for landing about three o'clock in the afternoon."

"And what's the name of the island?" asked Charles.

"Burhou."

"What a jolly name! It sounds full of pirates."

"Too dangerous a coast for them, my boy. Low, vicious rocks jutting out from it in every direction, and beyond, out to sea, the Casquets—more terrible rocks where many a ship has been wrecked, especially in the days before a lighthouse was built there. Even from here you can only get at the island in calm weather."

"It doesn't look far when you see it from the cliffs," said William.

"It isn't far, but look at the Swinge! It's full of swift currents and broken water racing in every direction. On calm days no one but a man who knows the currents could get you across—and if there's any sea running, nothing will induce anyone from this island to try it, so Robert says."

"The boat from Guernsey comes that way three times a week," objected Charles.

"That's a big boat," said Mr. Bailey, "and it's coming along with the main current, or against it, which is a far easier matter than trying to cross it. And that boat does not attempt the journey when it's very rough, and sometimes in winter doesn't turn up for a week. And when it arrives, it steams into a harbor, alongside a jetty, a very different thing from running up onto four foot of sandy shore with pointed rocks on either side, which is the only place of landing that Burhou has. No boat that was ever made could do that on a rough day."

"I don't think it sounds at all a nice place," said Mrs. Bailey, "I shall stop at home!"

"My dear!" expostulated her husband, "it will make a delightful expedition. On a calm day, there is no danger whatever, and on a rough day, no one will dream of going there."

"Oh, Daddy, you can't go without *us,*" said William reproachfully.

"Can't we? Your Mother and I want a peaceful afternoon together."

"Oh, no, no!" cried the Seven.

"We will be very good," promised Rose.

"And do everything you tell us," added Stella.

"And help you carry things," said Charles.

"And look after the babies and not let them worry you," said William.

"It is not usually the *babies* who worry us," put in Mrs. Bailey, pointedly.

William, thinking of his disastrous climb up the cliffs, blushed.

"Well, we can decide on all the details of our expedition tomorrow," interposed Mr. Bailey. "It may rain. So let us all enjoy ourselves today. Come along, William, and I'll render first aid to your hands."

Half an hour later Robert and the two eldest boys set out on their rabbit-trapping operations, William looking very smart and very self-conscious in a beautiful pair of new wash-leather gloves that fitted tidily over his bandages.

"Don't get them soiled," were his father's last words to him. "They are my one and only pair!"

"We.will go up the valley and set our traps," said Robert, as the three crossed the causeway. "Then we must leave them, and go round tonight, and see what we have caught."

"What shall we do all day?" asked Charles anxiously. "We have brought our lunch with us, you know."

"After we have set our traps, I want to go on over to the other side of the island to get a couple of fowls. There's a man lives in a fort over there who keeps a lot of poultry. Then we can collect a bit of wood and make a fire. I put a few potatoes in my pockets, and we can roast 'em. We might as well make a day of it."

"Oh, what fun!" exclaimed William, hopping about with excitement.

"Won't we have to go home in time for tea?" asked Charles, not yet sure of their good fortune.

"That's all right," said Robert. "I fixed it up with Matilda, and told her not to expect us till she saw us. There's not much she doesn't know about going for a day's rabbiting."

Robert's program was carried out with many glorious additions, and it was nearly nine o'clock that night before they returned, very tired, but glowing with excitement.

Mr. and Mrs. Bailey were standing at the court-yard door waiting for them, and directly the boys caught sight of them they broke into a run.

"We've got eleven rabbits," cried Charles, as soon as he was within shouting distance.

"We've left some traps set, and we are going again in the morning," shouted William.

"Robert says they are all young and fat."

"We set the traps ourselves."

"Robert showed us how to skin them, and we skinned one each."

"Just look at them! Aren't they beauties?"

"Oh, dear!" cried Mrs. Bailey. "Are they all dead?"

"They die at once," Charles assured her. "It all happens to them so quickly that they don't feel it, Robert says."

"Take them in to Matilda now," said Mr. Bailey. "She has supper all ready for you."

"We had a lot of the most lovely potatoes we ever tasted," said Charles. "But we're awfully hungry. Oh, we have had such a lovely day!"

"It was very kind of Robert to take you," said their mother. "Now run along, and when you've finished supper you must go straight to bed. It's very late, and you ought to have been asleep long ago."

"Did you notice my gloves?" asked Mr. Bailey, as the boys disappeared into the house.

"Well, yes, I did," admitted his wife.

"So did I," said Mr. Bailey, with ominous calm. "Any more horrible-looking objects I have seldom seen."

"Oh, Arthur! I was hoping you wouldn't notice them. When he has finished with them I will clean them thoroughly."

"When he has finished with them," said Mr. Bailey gloomily, "there will be nothing of them left to clean."

Violet

CHAPTER VII

THE DESERTED ISLAND

"THE glass is going down a trifle," announced Mr. Bailey the next morning, as he stood in the hall after breakfast and tapped the barometer.

"We've had a long spell of sunny weather," remarked his wife. "I suppose that all good things must come to an end some time."

"My dear, what a depressing sentiment! I'm rather looking forward to sitting snug in our fortress while the rain beats down, and the sea dashes against our rocky walls."

Mrs. Bailey shivered. "I daresay that it will be very pleasant, Arthur, though it sounds to me rather terrible. Meanwhile, I think that we had better postpone our visit to the island till the glass sets fair again, and get on with our unpacking."

"Barometers are not always right," objected Mr. Bailey cheerfully. "True, it may rain tomorrow, but just look at the blue sky today. The conditions are perfect, and I think it would be a thousand pities to put off our expedition."

"Going to have a change in the weather soon," said Robert, who had just come in to call the boys to go the round of their rabbit traps. "The sun rose very red and stormy, and just hark at them gulls!"

"I think it will be fine enough today," said Mr. Bailey with unshaken confidence, in spite of the warnings of the sun and the gulls. "Did you arrange for us to have the boat?"

"Yes," said Robert. "James can't come. He's got a job on, mending a roof, so I'm going along to fetch it."

"Can you manage it alone?"

Robert looked hurt. "My father was drowned at sea," he said, "and his father and grandfather before him. There's not many as knows as much about a boat as I do."

"Oh, well, that's all right," said Mr. Bailey hastily. "What time shall we start?"

"We shan't be able to land on the island till three because of the tide, and we ought to leave there about six. We couldn't get off in the boat much later than that."

"Is it rough there?" asked Mrs. Bailey.

" 'Tis when it blows," replied Robert. "But the trouble is, there isn't much of a landing place, and it's only safe at low tide anyway. In rough weather you can't land there at all, high tide or low tide, for months at a time."

"I'll go and see if those boys are ready," said Mr. Bailey.

"When we've got the rabbits I'll send 'em straight home, and go on for the boat. I'll bring her round about two."

"Very well, Robert. We'll be waiting for you on the landing stage here."

"What about the children?" asked Mrs. Bailey. "Shall we take them all with us?"

"I suppose so," replied her husband. "They'll be very much disappointed if we don't."

"Oh, dear!" exclaimed Mrs. Bailey suddenly. "I quite forgot that today is mail day. I must go up to the town to get a few things that I ordered fresh from Guernsey."

"The boat is due in about midday," said Robert.

"Then I doubt if I shall be back in time to go to the island with you, Arthur. But if not, don't wait for me. If there is time Robert can come back to fetch me, and I'll join you there."

"Hullo, Robert!" cried Charles, rushing in from the courtyard, "we didn't know you were here. I'll run and call William."

Two minutes later they were running along the causeway with Robert, on their way to the rabbit traps.

"I shall get ready now," said Mrs. Bailey. "It's a long walk into St. Anne's."

"I'll take the youngsters paddling among the rocks," said her husband. "I suppose it will be no good waiting lunch for you?"

"No, I'll have lunch somewhere in the town, and be back as soon as I can after my things come off the boat."

Mr. Bailey strolled away to collect the children, who were playing in the courtyard, and his wife went to get ready for her walk.

"Good-bye, Arthur," she said, when she came out a few minutes later. "Don't let the babies worry you."

"Rather not!" replied Mr. Bailey, with more conviction than he felt. "Good-bye."

The five stood on the causeway to wave her out of sight. After that they set about the morning's occupation of paddling and climbing among the pools, while Mr. Bailey sat on a low rock, with his feet in the water, and smoked a peaceful pipe. He was roused by shouts from Charles and William.

"We've got five more rabbits," they cried, as they came dashing up to him, "and Robert told us to take them to the outhouse and skin them."

"What a delightful job!" said their father. "I could find it in my heart to envy you."

"We shall have to hurry," said Charles. "We want to get them done before Robert comes back."

They ran off helter-skelter. Mr. Bailey finished his pipe and lit a second one, and was surprised to find how quickly the morning had gone when he saw Matilda at the door, and heard the bell for lunch, which she rang vigorously.

"We had a splendid morning," said Charles, as they all sat down to their meal, "but we haven't quite finished skinning the rabbits. I've done one, and I'm in the middle of another. William can't get on so quickly because of his gloves."

Mr. Bailey smoked a peaceful pipe.

"Gloves!" ejaculated Mr. Bailey in a horrified voice. "You don't mean to say you skinned rabbits with my gloves on, William?"

"I tried to, but they were rather in the way."

"I give them to you, William. I make you a free gift. I wish to think of them no longer as mine. They are yours. By the way, do any of you want to go to the island of Burhou this afternoon?"

"Oh, Daddy!" cried the Seven, in tones of ecstasy.

"All who want to go must be ready, in jerseys and coats, as soon as possible after lunch. Charles, I give you Maurice; William, your charge is Anthony; Rose, you see that Stella is ready; Violet, you can look after yourself."

So it happened that when Robert arrived at the landing stage soon after two o'clock, that he found the whole party, together with a large tea-basket prepared by Matilda, waiting for him.

"The postman is just coming up the causeway," he said. "The mail boat came in pretty punctual today. I saw her in the harbor as I was going along."

"Let's wait a minute to see what he's brought," said Mr. Bailey, walking off briskly to meet the postman.

There were several letters and papers, and a large registered parcel, with many massive red seals.

"What a lovely parcel!" exclaimed Violet. "Is it chocolates?"

Mr. Bailey was tearing it open excitedly.

"Hurrah! Something much better than chocolates!" he cried. "The first proofs of my 'Primitive Peoples.' I must look through them at once. I want to see how they have printed my diagrams on distribution and migration."

"But, Daddy, the boat is waiting," cried Charles.

"You can all go on with Robert, and I will follow later with your mother. Robert, you can land the children and return for us. Charles and William, you will be in charge of the babies till we come, so keep all together on the sands."

"May we paddle?" asked Rose.

"Yes, but you mustn't go farther than up to your knees. I suppose it's quite safe, isn't it, Robert?"

"Beautiful sands," Robert assured him. "Maybe they won't come to much harm there."

"They had better not! Now, get into the boat all of you, and sit quite still. Remember that Robert is the captain, and you must do exactly as he tells you."

"If they don't," said Robert, "I'll throw them overboard."

"We're off, we're off," shouted the Seven, as

Robert set the motor engine going and drew off from the landing stage.

"I want to be a sailor when I grow up," said Charles, as the boat ran swiftly through the waves and the sea rushed past them on either side.

The Six agreed with him emphatically.

"Why aren't you a sailor, Robert?" asked Rose.

"I was when I was a lad, but Matilda didn't like it. She doesn't understand the sea—she's a foreigner."

"I didn't know that," said William, in a slightly awed voice. "Is she Italian—or Spanish?"

"She's English—from Manchester. She never saw the sea till she came to Guernsey. She couldn't bear the idea of going back again by sea so, as she couldn't get there any other way, she stayed where she was— till I came along. We met at a Punch and Judy show on the beach."

"Were you Punch?" asked Stella.

"No, and she weren't Judy. But I was standing alongside of her, and you should have heard her laugh when Judy poked a stick in Punch's eye! So I laughed too, very hearty-like, and after that we both laughed, and after that of course I had to offer to see her home."

"Of course," agreed Charles, while Rose and Violet nodded assent. They were spellbound by these romantic reminiscences.

"But she had to come on the sea to come here," said Williams, who had been pondering over the matter for some time.

"She did," agreed Robert, "and I've never heard the last of it. I told her 'twas no distance to speak of, and always as calm as a millpond. And as it turned out 'twas the roughest crossing known for years, and lasted the best part of seven hours. She took on something cruel."

Robert lapsed into silence for a time as he steered the boat across the swift-flowing channel. Here the sea became rough and choppy, and the little vessel danced up and down as lightly as a cork on the waves. The children grew quiet, and sat huddled close together.

"Feeling a bit squeamish?" asked Robert, breaking the silence as they got into calmer waters. " 'Twill be worse than this, coming back. The wind's blowing up a bit fresher than I like. However, we're more than halfway across now. You can see the sands, and those posts sticking up there are by the landing place."

"I see a house," said Charles. "Does anyone live there?"

"Not now," answered Robert. "People did use to live there, but the young folk nowadays say it's too lonely. I mind the old fellow that was there when I was a lad. His name was Pitt—Jack Pitt—lived there all alone he did, and never saw a soul for months at a stretch. And before him was Old Ned the Miser."

"Did he save a lot of money?" asked Charles.

" 'Twas said he had piles and piles of it; but if he had he hid it well, for it's never been found to this day. 'Old Ned's Nest-Egg' they call it. When my grandfather was a lad they used to go over and hunt for it now and then; but as nobody ever found a trace of it folks got tired of looking."

"What did he eat?" asked Anthony.

"Rabbits," said Robert. "The wonder was he didn't turn into one himself, so they said."

"Why don't you live there, Robert?" suggested Charles. "Is it a nice house?"

" 'Tis a good house enough, and anyone could have it for the asking. But I couldn't get Matilda there. She's made a vow never to set foot in a boat again so long as she lives. Now don't you talk to me

no more. We're coming to a mighty ticklish
bit."

The long, low island rose, gray and wild-looking,
before them. To right and left it sloped down and
ended in sharp and cruel-looking rocks that ran out
into the sea till only their jagged tops were visible.
Facing them was a square-built, white cottage,
flanked by rising ground overgrown with gorse; and
immediately below it was a lovely stretch of golden
sand. At one end of this were a few posts that did for
a rough landing stage. After a good deal of
manœuvring Robert stopped the engine, and the boat
glided slowly alongside. With a swift movement he
flung a rope over one of the upright posts and
made fast.

"You two boys get off first," he said to Charles and
William, "and then you can give a hand to the others.
I'll hold her close up, and when I say 'Jump,' you
jump, and jump smart."

The boys did as they were told, and in a very few
moments all the Seven were on dry land. Robert
carried Maurice on to the sands, and sat down.

"I must have a pipe," he said, "before I go back
along for your Pa and Ma. 'Tis a terrible hard job
bringing in that boat single-handed. I couldn't do it

if 'twere much rougher than 'tis now. The currents hereabouts are cruel shifty."

"Do many boats pass along here?" asked Charles.

"No more than can help it. The one as brings the mail does it pretty regular, but then the captain knows every inch of it as well as you know your A B C. If he didn't he'd strike a rock the very first go off. Many and many's the boat that has sunk hereabouts and t'other side, out toward the Casquets. They always keep some food and firing in the cottage for sailors that get shipwrecked on this island. Once they get washed up on it in stormy weather, there's no getting them off till it grows calm again."

"Have you ever been shipwrecked, Robert?" inquired William.

"No, but I've known them that has been. Six years ago come Christmas there was a French sailing-boat that struck the rocks in a storm—got blown straight on to them, she did. Five of her crew managed to get ashore, and they lived here for six weeks before we could get to them. James and me got to them first in this very boat, and you never saw such a lot of wild savages as they looked."

"Did they draw lots and eat each other?" asked

Charles, while all the others listened with rapt attention.

"No, they was all too tough for that—no more fit for food than old boots. They ate up all the food there was in Castaway Cottage, as we call it, and thinned out the rabbits pretty considerable. They were that glad to see me and James when we came along that they were jumping about like grass-hoppers on this very spot, and all talking at once. And their hair and whiskers were that thick and long that James and me reckoned that we might get a good price for them if we could get them to the Zoo."

"And did you?" inquired Rose breathlessly.

"No such luck! We took them off, and there was the Governor and a big crowd waiting to meet us on the quay. They had got out the band, too, and everyone cheered, and you never heard such a hulla-baloo. We all had dinner at the Governor's house, and the Governor made a speech, and said he would have given me and James a gold medal each if he'd had any handy. We ought to have had one by rights, because all those French chaps kissed us. 'Twas a cruel hard thing when you come to think of it, for they hadn't washed or shaved for six weeks or more."

"Didn't they have any water?" asked Violet.

"There's plenty of water, but if you ask me I think

they was glad of the excuse to do without. There's a spring up there beyond those rocks, and an old well by the cottage. Just look at them clouds blowing up. I think I'd best take you all home again with me."

"No, no, no," shouted the Seven. "Daddy said we were to paddle."

"Well, the sooner I get off the sooner I'll be back. Now, mind you don't go wandering about, because we shan't have no time to spare for sending out search parties looking for the lost. You lads come along and help me get off."

He knocked out his pipe, and put it in his pocket, and then led the way down to the boat.

"Now, then, my lads, you hold on to this rope and hold on tight. And when I say, 'let go,' let go sharp."

The boys followed his directions with great vigor. The engine was started, the rope was cast loose, and very soon Robert was going full-speed ahead away from the Seven. They watched his little boat get smaller and smaller in the distance, and heard the cheerful pop-pop of the engine grow fainter. Then they all turned and went back to the sands, and soon their joyous shouts and laughter broke the silence of that desolate beach, and set all the seagulls screaming round them.

CHAPTER VIII

THE STORM RISES

WHEN Mrs. Bailey arrived at the Fort, laden with parcels, it was nearly three o'clock. As she entered the courtyard she caught sight of her husband seated on one of the ramparts, apparently absorbed in a book.

"Arthur!" she cried in amazement, "I thought you had gone to Burhou. Where are the children?"

"Oh, they're gone on," replied Mr. Bailey, barely looking up from the pages on which he was so intent. "Do come here and see the mess they've made of this diagram. I particularly told them——"

"Arthur, what are you talking about?" said his wife, who by this time had joined him on the rampart. "You surely didn't let the children go alone?"

"Not alone, they went with Robert. They're all right. Now do look——"

"But when are they coming back? Did they go in the boat?"

"Yes, of course they did, dear. We were just starting off when the postman came, and brought the proofs of my book. Do just look at——"

"Arthur, I must know about the children first. When are they coming back?"

"They're not coming back," said Mr. Bailey. "You remember when I sent off my manuscript, I told them——"

"Not coming back, Arthur? What do you mean? Here, give me those proofs. I won't listen to another word about them till you explain what has happened."

Mr. Bailey reluctantly tore his gaze away from his precious papers.

"I told Robert to take the children to Burhou," he said, "and put them safely on the sands, and then return for you and me. You arranged for him to return for you, you know."

"But I thought you would be with the children, Arthur. I should never have dreamt of letting them stay on the island all alone—such a bare, wild-looking place!" She gave a little shiver.

"My dear," said Mr. Bailey soothingly, "they're quite happy and safe. Robert says the sands are good, and if he says they're good, you may depend on it that they're perfect.   It's only a matter of an hour or two, and Rose and the boys are quite capable of looking after the younger ones."

"I can't help remembering how they all got shut into that black storehouse—and the fright we had when William got stuck on those awful rocks. I——"

"They must learn," interrupted Mr. Bailey, "and the only way to learn is by experience.   Neither of those two mishaps is likely to occur again.   Children should be encouraged to use their own common sense, and not to be entirely dependent on their elders."

"I agree with you up to a certain point, Arthur, but when it comes to endangering their lives I——"

"Endangering their lives!" repeated Mr. Bailey in a shocked voice.   "My dear, there is no question of that.   You are taking far too serious a view of the whole thing.   Robert will be back for us very soon now—in fact he may be here at any moment."

"He's not in sight yet," said Mrs. Bailey, looking anxiously out to sea in the direction of the island.

"I mean that we may see him coming at any moment.   The crossing takes a very short time.   At most they'll be alone for about an hour, playing about on

very safe sands. Why, we often lose sight of them
for two or three hours, and never worry about them."

"That's true; but we know this place now, and
we know nothing about the island at all."

"That proves what I say," cried Mr. Bailey
triumphantly. "The danger lies entirely in your imagination. Now, I imagine them happily engaged
in digging holes and building castles, while you seem
to imagine all sorts of accidents befalling them, none
of which are at all likely to happen."

"Perhaps you are right, Arthur. But you must
remember that I thought you were with them, and it
gave me quite a shock to find you here, and the children gone."

"It never occurred to you that *I* might be in danger
left all alone *here!*" said Mr. Bailey jestingly.
"Now, don't worry any more. Just come and sit
here, and give me your advice about these diagrams.
I must have them perfectly clear."

Mrs. Bailey sat down beside him, and he was at
once absorbed again in problems of style, and
printers' misunderstandings of his meaning. He
explained his diagrams in relation to his maps, and
his wife listened with all the concentration she could
muster. But her eyes kept straying toward the

island, and she longed for the sight of the returning boat, and the sound of its noisy little motor-
engine.

"Isn't Robert gone a long time?" she said to her
husband at length.

Mr. Bailey looked at his watch. "Good gracious!"
he exclaimed in tones of amazement. "It's nearly
half-past three. I had no idea it was so late. He
must be staying with the children, showing them
round a bit. I certainly expected he would be back
for us before this. He probably thought there was
no hurry. You remember he said it would be all
right there till six o'clock, and he is sure to allow
plenty of time."

"Yes, but we're going to have tea there, Arthur.
Didn't they take it with them?"

"Yes, Matilda packed it up, and I put it in the
boat. Look, there he is! That black speck in a line
with that high rock!"

Mr. Bailey stood pointing, and they watched in
silence for several minutes. The sea, which that
morning had been so calm and blue, now looked gray
and choppy, and great black clouds were banking up
in the west.

"It's coming this way right enough," he said at

length, "though it's not on a very direct course. I'm rather puzzled by the way it tacks about, but probably there are many rocks to be avoided."

"Perhaps something has gone wrong with the steering gear," suggested Mrs. Bailey anxiously. "Oh, I wish he would be quick! Look, the sun has gone in, and those clouds seem dreadfully threatening. And the sea is ever so much rougher than it was even a few minutes ago."

"We may have a slight shower," said Mr. Bailey lightly, though he began to look rather worried. "I will go and fetch your coat."

He strode off into the Fort, and was very soon back again, carrying a load of coats and rugs. The boat was now making straight for them, and was rapidly drawing near.

"That's Robert, all right. Be ready to jump in, and we will set out at once."

Mrs. Bailey needed no bidding. They stood together on the little landing stage, and in less time than had seemed possible a few minutes earlier Robert was gliding up alongside. His face was begrimed with oil from the engine and, to Mrs. Bailey's anxious eyes, his face wore a look of strain.

"You're very late," shouted Mr. Bailey, jumping

into the boat, followed closely by his wife, "why didn't you come back earlier?"

"I've had a terrible time getting here," returned Robert. "The Swinge is running cruel. We shan't be able to make Burhou tonight."

"What do you mean?" cried Mr. Bailey. "We can't leave the children there alone. We've *got* to get there, Swinge or no Swinge!"

" 'Tisn't possible. No one could do it—it's madness to try. I've never seen a storm blow up more wild. The sea knows what's coming."

"Do you mean you don't *want* to go?" asked Mr. Bailey sternly.

"I'm only warning you," growled Robert. "I don't mind drowning particular—it's in the family and seems natural-like."

"Do you think there is any risk of drowning if we go?" asked Mr. Bailey, looking him squarely in the face.

Robert shook his head. "Risk?" he said. "It's pretty near a certainty."

Mr. Bailey looked out to sea, and suddenly realized the desperate truth of Robert's words.

"Alice," he said quickly, turning to his wife, "jump out at once. Robert and I are going to the

island. If we don't come back tonight you'll know
we are staying there with the children. Don't worry
about us."

"I'm coming with you," said his wife sharply.

"You're not. Jump out quickly."

"I'm coming with you," she repeated. "If not,
I'll get out the rowing boat and follow you. Quick,
make up your mind. We are wasting time."

She stood up, and looked at her husband with
determination in her eyes, and he knew that her mind
was made up.

"Set her at it, Robert. We'll do it," he said.

Without a word Robert turned the boat and steered
for the little island again. The wind caught them
sideways, and they rocked violently in the choppy
water. Mrs. Bailey sat in the bow, with her face set
and pale, looking straight before her at the receding
Fort, while her husband turned and faced the channel
that swept before them. Straight ahead he could see
the white-capped waves racing along with the current, and the spray dashing against the rocks that
rose here and there out of the sea. Rain began to
fall in a torrential downpour, and the waves washed
into the boat continuously. Robert, who was standing tense and alert at the steering wheel, suddenly

stooped and picked up a bucket which lay close to his hand, and held it out to Mr. Bailey.

"Better bale her out while you can," he shouted. " 'Twon't be for long by the look of it."

Mr. Bailey seized the bucket and began to bale out the sea from the boat with might and main. Very soon he threw off his mackintosh coat, and worked in his shirt-sleeves. He was drenched to the skin, water streamed down his hair into his eyes, and he tasted the salt of the sea in his mouth as he drew his breath in gasps. In spite of all his efforts he could not keep the boat clear, and very soon he was ankle-deep in water which grew deeper every minute. He ceased a moment from his task, and threw a wild glance ahead. Through the blinding rain and spray he saw the turmoil around him and the racing waves before, and he recognized defeat.

"You were right, Robert" he shouted, "we can't do it. Turn her back."

Robert shook his head and shouted something, but the only words that reached Mr. Bailey were "too late." Then he gave a backward look at the Fort, and with a mighty pull at the wheel turned the boat half round, into the teeth of a wind that was fast becoming a gale.

"Hold tight," he yelled, as the current caught the boat and heeled her over till her bottom stood up at right angles. For a moment it seemed impossible that she could right herself again, then she came over, steadied herself, and took a leap forward. She was now half-full of water.

"Bail her out!" yelled Robert. "We're sinking."

Mr. Bailey obeyed the order as one possessed. He worked till his breath came in panting sobs, and he could neither see nor hear. His brain became numb, and but one thought filled his mind: he must clear the boat of water. How long his frenzied effort lasted he never knew; but suddenly he felt the bucket pulled from his hands, and he half fell and was half pushed on to the seat. He brushed the water from his eyes, and dimly saw his wife wielding the bucket steadily and swiftly, and, looming up beyond her, the walls of the Fort. Then he knew that Robert had succeeded in turning the boat, and that they were now heading for home. Yet they were still some distance off, and he wondered stonily if they would ever reach it. The boat, it was certain, could not be kept afloat much longer. He himself was a strong swimmer, but he knew that his wife could never make any headway in such a sea, and Robert he guessed, from his knowledge of most fishermen and boatmen, would sink at once.

He got up and went over to him. "Can you swim?" he shouted.

Robert shook his head vigorously, but never took his gaze from the Fort, as he guided the boat with unfaltering hands.

Mr. Bailey took the bucket from his wife, and, without a pause, went on bailing.

"Take off your shoes and coat," he cried to her. "We may have to swim for it."

She did as he told her; then stood looking at the Fort, and at the men. She wondered whether they would ever reach the landing stage, against which the waves were now dashing, but she felt neither hope nor fear. All her mind and heart had been bent on getting to her children and, now that the boat was turned away from them, she cared nothing for what the immediate future might hold.

Though he bailed without ceasing, the water gained steadily on Mr. Bailey; yet the boat struggled on, every minute sinking lower and lower into the sea, but at the same time getting a little nearer the Fort. Once as he swung out his bucket he caught a warning look from Robert and saw his lips move, though he heard no sound. He stepped nearer.

"We can't stop at the landing stage," Robert bawled in his ear, "but as I come past it, jump."

Mr. Bailey nodded and when within a few yards of the steps he dropped his bucket and, going over to his wife, caught her up in his arms. He carried her to the boat's side, and stood so that her feet rested on the edge.

"As we pass the steps, jump," he cried to her, and a moment later the boat lurched toward the landing stage on the top of a wave, and crashed against it. In that second he let go his hold on her, and she jumped clear. As the boat was drawn back by the wash of the wave, he saw her fingers grip one of the steps while her feet searched for another. He saw her fingers slip from the wet stone, then she stumbled forward, and a wave carried her upwards. The wave retreated, and left her scrambling up the steps to safety. As he uttered a prayer of thanksgiving he felt the boat sinking under him, and turned to Robert.

"Kick off your boots," he shouted, "and try to float, and I'll get you to shore."

He saw Robert stoop to do his bidding, and he himself quickly followed suit. The next moment they were in the seething water.

When Mr. Bailey rose to the surface he could see

no sign of Robert. The waves were running so high that it was impossible to remain still in one spot, and he had no notion in which direction he should look for him. He swam round as nearly as he could in circles. He shouted, "Robert, Robert," but, when he listened for an answering shout, heard nothing but the dashing of waves over the rocks.

As he was beginning to despair he saw a hand rising above a wave only a few yards away. He swam frantically to the spot, and flung himself at a dim shadow under the water. It was Robert; and in a moment he had grabbed him by the hair, and was holding the head of his unconscious companion out of the water as high as he could manage.

The tide was running along the shore, and he swiftly considered his best course of action. If he could keep Robert afloat while the sea carried them round the next headland of rock he thought he might be able, by a desperate effort, to get on the lee side in the bay beyond, where the current would be far less strong, and he would then have the chance of getting his burden on to a sandy beach.

He proceeded to put this plan into action. With surprising swiftness they were swept along, till they came level with the outstanding line of rocks. Suddenly Robert spoke.

"This is a terrible place," he remarked in a sepulchral voice.

Mr. Bailey, in other circumstances, could have laughed with glee, so glad was he to know that Robert still lived, and that it was not the body of a drowned man that he was trying to save.

"Hang on to my shoulder," he shouted, as he turned his face to the shore, and swam with his mightiest breast-stroke. Robert obeyed his instructions with automatic precision, and after a few minutes Mr. Bailey, who had marked his position in line with a certain rock, saw that they were making headway. Little by little, inch by inch, they got nearer in, till suddenly—or so it seemed to the nearly exhausted swimmer—they were out of the sweeping current and into water that was, by contrast, still. With a last effort he set out to cover that remaining distance to the shore, till he found that he could just manage to stand.

"It's all right, Robert, stand up," he gasped, and felt his shoulder released as he lapsed into unconsciousness.

The next thing he knew was that he was lying on

the shore, being rubbed roughly all over by Robert. A great feeling of thankfulness stole over him till full consciousness returned, and with it the thought of his children.

"The children!" he cried aloud, "I must get to them somehow."

Stella

CHAPTER IX

CASTAWAY COTTAGE

HAVING seen Robert safely off in his boat from the landing stage of Burhou, the Seven ran back to the sands and their own amusements. They dug several holes and watched how rapidly they were filled by the incoming tide; and they built castles, on which they stood till a wave bigger than the rest forced them to retire from strongholds that were soon washed away in ruins. So busy were they that none of them noticed the black clouds that were fast rolling up from the horizon, till a few drops of rain began to fall.

"Hallo!" exclaimed Charles, "if it isn't beginning to rain! I hope it won't come to much."

"I should think there's going to be a pretty bad storm," said William. "Just look at the sky!"

"We had better get into shelter," suggested Rose, "though I don't know where we shall get any. There are no trees in sight, and no caves."

"Castaway Cottage, of course," shouted Charles. "Come on, you babies, let's run for it."

"What about our coats and the tea-basket?" asked Rose.

"We'll take them along with us," said Charles. "There's no sense in letting them get soaked."

They gathered up the things, and ran as fast as they could to the cottage, for the rain was now coming down in earnest. William was the first to reach the door, which was at the back of the house. He lifted the latch and, to his great joy, it opened easily, and the Seven were soon inside, laughing, and breathless, and all talking at once.

"Oh, what fun!"

"Fancy being in Castaway Cottage all by ourselves!"

"What a dear little house!"

"I hope Daddy and Mummy will be a long time coming!"

"We're all rather wet," said Rose suddenly, in a very practical tone of voice. "I think we should take off our jerseys and shake them out."

"I don't see that will do any good," objected William, "and I'm not a bit wet."

"I think we ought to make the babies do it," decided Charles. "Now then, you babies, off with your jerseys!"

He seized Maurice, and proceeded to assist him with great vigor, while Rose and William did the same for the others, amid much laughter and cries of remonstrance. There were tremendous shakings of clothes and of children, and eventually all were dressed again.

"That was a good piece of work," exclaimed Charles. "I'm hot all over."

"Now let's explore the cottage," said William, and the suggestion met with loud cries of approval.

The room they stood in was low and square, with one small window. It had evidently been used as a kitchen at some time, for in one corner of it stood a rusty oil-stove, and on a shelf some old crockery was piled.   A frying-pan, a kettle, and two sauce-pans hung from nails driven into the wall, and a small deal table and a few old sugar-boxes completed the furnishing.   Against one wall was a large cup-board.

"What a dear little room!" exclaimed Stella, jump-ing about with excitement.

"Yes," said Charles, "everything for use.   I won-der where this leads?"

As he spoke he opened another door, and there was a general stampede as the children trooped through it and found themselves in a big front room, facing the sea.   It had two windows, and against the panes the rain was pouring in sheets, so that it was impos-sible to see what lay outside.

"I hope Daddy and Mummy will come here to look for us," said Violet anxiously.   "Do you think they'll be sure to find us?"

"Of course they will," Charles assured her.   "It's the first place they'll look for us.   Anyhow, Robert will, because he told us about it."

The room was very bare and held little to interest the Seven.   A stained deal table stood before one of the windows, and folded up against the wall were a few old camp-stools.   The fireplace was red with rust, and filled with old newspapers, and a three-year-old almanac lay on the mantelpiece.

"Here's another door," cried Stella, who had been wandering round the room with the rest, "and inside there's some dear little stairs."

There was a rush to examine this find, and the next minute they were all climbing up the "dear little stairs." They arrived at the top in a room exactly like the one they had just left, save that its ceiling was sloping and low—so low that Charles could touch it with his fingers when he stood on tiptoe. A door stood open between this room and a back one built over the kitchen. In the front room were some rough shelves and a cupboard; in the back one a pile of matting and some striped rugs were stacked on a low chest.

"I wonder whom these things belong to?" said Violet.

"Why, they're for shipwrecked sailors, of course," said Charles. "I wish some would turn up while we're here."

"Perhaps they will, if Mummy and Daddy come a bit late," said William hopefully. "It's pretty rough. I wonder if Robert would call this a gale?"

The wind howled round the house, and the rain fell in torrents.

"No," scoffed Charles. "He might say there was a bit of a breeze blowing."

"And that it had turned out a bit damp," added William.

"What ever should we do if a shipwrecked sailor came up those stairs?" asked Violet in an awed voice.

"I should say 'Bo,'" said Stella.

"Then he'd run you through without further parley, with his cutlass," said William. "The proper way to address a shipwrecked sailor is 'Hullo, mate'!"

"I want my tea," interrupted Maurice, who was getting rather tired.

"There's a table downstairs in the front room," said Charles. "Let's go and unpack the baskets and lay tea, and by that time I expect Daddy and Mummy will be here."

This suggestion was received with delight, and the Seven clattered downstairs again, and were soon busily engaged in laying out the good things Matilda had packed up for them.

"What a topping tea!" exclaimed William, as they

unwrapped several packets of sandwiches, a large current cake, some sponge-cake with jam in it, and ten bananas. There was also a bottle of milk, tea in a thermos flask, and some spoons and knives.

"I wish they would be quick," said Rose, and all the others echoed her wish.

"It's getting dark already," said Charles. "I wonder what the time is."

"It must be getting late, I think. I wonder if Mummy would like us to begin tea," suggested Rose.

"I think she would," said William emphatically, and as everyone agreed heartily, they were soon seated on stools round the table, thoroughly enjoying their meal.

The rain still beat ceaselessly against the window panes, the wind still howled down the chimney, and it grew so dark that the children could see each other but dimly.

Charles got up and went to the window; then he walked into the kitchen, and began to rummage about in the cupboard.

"William," he called out presently, "come and help me with this lamp a moment, will you?"

William joined him, and found him wrestling with an old hurricane lamp, that he had found on a shelf together with a tin box containing a dozen boxes of matches.

"Hold the bottom of it while I try to lift the glass up," he said, "it's a little rusty. It's got some oil in it, so be careful."

With some difficulty they succeeded in opening the lamp, and Charles put a light to the wick.

"William," he said in a low voice, "do you hear the sea?"

"Rather!" replied William. "I'm not deaf!"

"It's a storm. I don't think Daddy and Mummy will ever be able to get here in the boat tonight."

"I thought of that a long time ago," said William. "What shall we do?"

"Well, we are really shipwrecked. If we hadn't the babies with us it would be no end of a joke. I think we'd better tell Rose."

He called Rose, and in a hoarse whisper announced his belief that they were castaways in real earnest.

"What fun!" exclaimed Rose. Then, as she listened to the roar and clatter of wind and rain and sea, she added, "I do hope that Daddy and Mummy won't try to come tonight. They'll get very wet. And we're really quite all right here."

They were castaways in real earnest.

"What about the babies? They'll set up an awful howl!"

"No, they won't," said Rose with decision. "If we pretend it's a game they'll love it. I'll tell Violet first. You go in and tell her I want her, and then stay with the others till we come."

The boys carried out this plan, and played with the little ones till they were joined by the two girls, who danced in, looking very excited.

"What do you think, babies!" cried Rose. "We're all going to sleep tonight in this dear little house."

"Is Mummy coming?" asked Anthony.

"No, not tonight. It's too wet. I expect she'll be here to breakfast in the morning. We're going to sleep upstairs all in a row. And we've got to make our own beds."

"I want to go home to Mummy," announced Maurice stoutly.

"You're going to have a lovely bed on the floor," said Charles.

"And when you're in bed I'll give you another banana," added Rose with sudden inspiration.

"A whole one?" asked Maurice.

"Yes, a whole one, so come along. It's bed-time now. There are three bananas left, so Stella and Anthony can have one each, too."

They all trooped upstairs, Charles going first with the lantern. It cast strange shadows on the walls and ceiling, and for a moment his heart quailed.

"Hurry along, Charles," called William gruffly, "we're coming close behind you and we're treading on your tail!"

Charles pulled himself together, and carried his lantern to one of the windows.

"We'll leave the light here," he said, setting it down on the ledge, "to guide Daddy and Mummy in case they come."

"I think we'd better save the oil," said William in a far-reaching whisper. "Remember what Robert said about those French shipwrecked sailors—six weeks, you know!"

"Right you are, William. Perhaps we'd better all go to bed together now."

"Shall we undress?" asked Maurice.

"No," decided Rose, "let's spread out the mats and rugs, and see how many there are."

This was no sooner said than done, and Charles announced that there were eight mats and nine rugs.

"I think we'd better have a blanket each," he said, "and roll up in it. The mats will be our nice soft mattresses, and we'll all fit in together, like sardines.

And when you're ready I'll cover you over with the other two rugs, and slip in afterwards."

"Come along then, sardines," cried Rose, and one by one the babies were rolled round like mummies, and laid on the mats.

"We haven't said our prayers," said Anthony.

"Then get up and say them," said Rose. "We may as well say them all together."

The babies were got up again, and they all knelt down together, and repeated their prayers aloud.

"You do look funny," said Stella, when they had finished. "I wish Mummy was here!"

Could Mrs. Bailey have seen her children just then she would surely have wept over them: seven kneeling figures, each wrapped in a dark blanket, and each looking very solemn in the dim light of the lantern —and on the whitewashed wall seven shapeless shadows, very still.

"Now, into bed all of you," cried Rose, jumping up as quickly as her wrappings allowed. "We'll lie like sandwiches—a little one between two big ones."

"Yes," agreed William, "and I'll be at one end, and Charles can be at the other."

They lay down, with many amazed exclamations about the hardness of the mats. And when they were settled Charles spread the two extra rugs over them, and put out the lantern. Then he slipped into his end of the row, and very soon heard the regular breathing of the tired children. He lay for some time listening, and then he, too, slept.

In spite of the hardness of their strange bed, it was long past their usual waking-time before there was any movement among the Seven on the following morning. Rose was the first to open her eyes, and it was some time before she remembered where she was. She sat up on her mat and yawned.

"I wonder what time it is!" she exclaimed, "wake up, all of you! I'm sure it's time to get up."

All the children began to stir, and Charles jumped up and ran to the window. The rain had ceased, but the wind was howling round the cottage in great gusts, and out at sea the white-capped waves were rushing madly. They dashed high over the rocks of the island and the spray and foam were blown inland like thistledown.

"Oh, what a morning!" he cried, drawing a deep breath. "It's perfectly wonderful."

"Daddy and Mummy will never be able to get across to us today," said William, who now stood by his side at the window.

The babies set up a loud cry.

"I want Mummy to come," wailed Anthony.

"And I want Mummy, too," sobbed Maurice.

"Now don't cry," said Charles, soothingly. "You don't want Mummy and Daddy to come out on such a rough day, and get blown into the sea."

Rose turned the conversation quickly.

"What about breakfast?" she asked. "I feel very empty."

"So do I," said William, and the others agreed heartily.

"We really ought to get some water first," said Rose. "You all look as if you needed a wash, and I'm sure I do, too."

"I know what we'll do," cried Charles. "You girls stay here with the babies, Rose, and stop their howling, and William and I'll go round and try to find a tap somewhere. Robert said there was plenty of water."

"Will you promise not to be long?" asked Rose.

"We'll be as quick as ever we can," Charles assured her. "Come along, William."

The boys rushed eagerly downstairs, leaving Rose as she was comforting the younger ones by the promise of a story.

"There's no water inside the house," said Charles, glancing round the kitchen as they clattered through it. "We must look for the well that Robert said was near by."

A gust of wind caught them as they opened the door, and they shut it behind them with difficulty. They struggled round the cottage, holding on to each other as they were buffeted about, and laughing heartily the while, till they found themselves again at the cottage door, flushed and breathless.

"Oh, what fun!" exclaimed William. "Isn't it topping!"

Charles agreed, but then quickly bethought himself of their quest.

"We must find the water," he gasped. "Let's go round again and search for it."

Once more they set out, this time eagerly scanning the rough ground round about for any sign of a well. It was very wild and bare, here and there overgrown with coarse grass, and here and there strewn with stones and small rocks. Nothing else met their eyes till they turned the third corner, and then, about fifty yards away, they spied two wooden posts, standing upright.

Both boys gave a shout.

"That may be it," cried Charles. "Let's hang on to each other, and we'll go and explore."

The wind whistled in their ears, and the sea spray stung their faces, as they clasped hands and struggled along with heads down. They gave a whoop of delight as they came up to the posts, and saw that their guess had been correct. Between the posts was the well, and round one of them was fastened a rusty chain, the end of which hung down.

"I wonder where the tap is—the one you told Rose we might find?" grinned William.

"Don't be silly, William. I only *said* a 'tap'."

"I know you did. Don't apologize. I hope there's a bucket anyhow. I'll lie down and pull the chain, and you hold on to my legs."

He lay down and looked into the well.

"Do you see any water?" asked Charles anxiously.

"Yes, it looks pretty black too."

He began slowly to draw up the chain, helped by Charles.

"It's very heavy. There's something at the end of it, and if it's a bucket it must be full of something."

"Full of water, of course," said Charles. "Heave-ho!"

With much heavy panting, and many exclamations

and orders and counter-orders, they drew up the weight into the daylight, and landed a bucket that was half-full of water.

"Hurrah!" shouted Charles. "That was good work. Now we've got to get it home."

They unhooked the bucket and, each taking one side of the handle, stumbled back to the house, half blown along by the wind.

"Lucky we had the wind behind us!" exclaimed Charles, as they arrived at the cottage. "We've spilt a good lot of the water, but there's still a little left."

Entering the cottage they slammed the door and shouted for Rose, who flew downstairs, followed by the rest of the Seven.

"Is that all you've got—all this time!" she cried, looking into the bucket.

The boys looked crestfallen.

"It's awfully difficult to get any at all," said Charles. "You go and have a try. There's plenty down the well."

Rose was quickly repentant.

"I'm so glad you found it," she said. "But you did seem to be gone such a long time. I think the babies are hungry."

There was a chorus of agreement, punctuated by a few sobs.

"Well, go and wash," said Charles, who began to look rather worried. "William and I will see if we can find something for breakfast."

"We must manage without soap," said Rose, "and I will show you how to wash your faces with your hands—as rabbits and cats do with their paws."

Here was a game that appealed to the younger children, and they were soon gathered round the bucket, splashing about with squeals of delight.

"Come along, William," said Charles. "I do hope there's something to eat in the cupboard. Let's drag the table over here, and turn out everything on to it."

"Let's find something to eat first, and eat it," suggested William, "and feed all this crowd. Then we shall have a little peace and be able to sort things out."

"Good egg!" agreed Charles.

"Oh, Charles," cried Stella, "have you found some eggs?"

"No, of course he hasn't, silly," cried William. "Haven't you ever heard of an egg that's not an egg? You ought to go to school."

"We'll play at school after breakfast," suggested

Rose tactfully, as she showed Maurice how to shake his hands dry.

"There are dozens of tins of food here," murmured Charles from the cupboard.

"Trot them out quickly," cried William. "I hope there's sardines."

"This says it's kippered herring," said Charles, holding out a tin in an attractive-looking wrapper. "I expect it's delicious."

"Are there any bones in them?" asked Rose. "We don't want the babies to choke."

"We'll open the tin and see. I wonder where the opener is! There must be one somewhere. They couldn't expect shipwrecked sailors to have such a thing in their pockets!"

William, who was busily looking on all the shelves, suddenly gave a whoop of delight.

"Here's one, among all these old knives. Now then, Charles, do hurry up."

"And be careful," put in Rose. "It's fatal to cut yourself with tin. Mummy always says so."

At the end of several minutes Charles, helped by endless advice and criticism from the onlookers, had made only a very small opening.

"I had no idea that tins were such a bother to

open," he exclaimed at last, pausing for a moment to take breath.

"Don't do any more," implored William, "or we shan't have breakfast till tea-time. Poke out the stuff with a knife."

This suggestion was followed, and very soon a pile of minced kipper was heaped on a plate.

"What about bread?" asked Rose.

"The baker hasn't called yet, ma'am," said William.

"There's a packet of sandwiches and some cake that we saved last night for Daddy and Mummy," cried Charles. "It isn't much, but it will be better than nothing. Now, you all go into the dining room, and my mate and I will serve breakfast. We're butlers."

"What are we?" inquired Stella.

"You are lords and ladies. Tootle along."

There was a rush to the front room, and the boys were left by themselves. William got seven tin plates from a shelf, which he placed in a row on the table, after giving each a wipe with his sleeve, and Charles proceeded to divide their shares with the most careful exactitude.

"Do you think we should all have the same?" he

asked, "or do you think the babies should have less because they are smaller?"

"I'll ask Rose," volunteered William hopefully.

Rose gave it as her opinion that they should all have the same.

"There won't be much anyhow," she said, "and if we all share alike no one can grumble."

With much ceremony the two butlers brought in the seven plates, one by one, and the children fell to ravenously.

"There's no second helpings, my lords and ladies," warned Charles, "and no second course. So eat slowly and spin it out."

"Ought butlers to have breakfast with lords and ladies?" asked Stella.

"We live in the olden days," said Charles. "You ought to read *Beric the Briton.*"

"I wish we had *Robinson Crusoe* here to read," said William. "We might get no end of tips from him."

"The most important thing is to know what day it is," said Charles. "Robinson Crusoe kept a count of them by cutting notches on a stick—do you remember, William?"

"Rather! He got it wrong too, because one day he was too ill to know anything about it."

"We had better get a stick and start directly after breakfast," said Charles. "What day is it today?"

"Wednesday," said Rose promptly.

"No, it isn't," declared William, "it's Thursday. It was Wednesday yesterday. I know that because Matilda goes and does her shopping on Tuesday, and she went out the day before."

"Yes, but she changed her day this week," said Charles. "I heard her tell Mother that she wanted to go out to tea somewhere. I think it's Friday."

"I don't see that it matters much what day it is," said Rose with a cheerful grin. "Couldn't we begin today, and call it Monday? Then we could count up the weeks and the months and the years just the same, and be able to tell about how old we are by the time we are rescued."

"I want some more," Maurice interrupted, turning his empty plate upside-down on the table.

"We'll have our lunch nice and early," promised Charles. "You play about here, and William and I will do the cooking."

"You must get some more water first," said Rose, "and we'll wash up. The babies can help."

"Our plates are quite clean," protested William. "If we have to keep on getting water we shan't have time to do any cooking today."

"Come along, William," said Charles. "We may as well get it over. We shall want some water anyhow, in case we find anything to cook for our lunch."

"I expect we'll have to draw lots, and boil each other," said William. "Your head would be nice and tender, Charles, though there's not much in it."

With these barbed words he opened the door and rushed out quickly, closely followed by Charles carrying the bucket, and the slam of the door behind them shook the little cottage to its foundations.

CHAPTER X

HARD WORK

ROSE was worried. The babies cried and would not listen to stories, nor play any of the games that she racked her brains to suggest. They wanted "Mummy" and they refused to be comforted. Also after their light breakfast, they were still hungry.

"I wish the boys would be quick," she said to Violet for the twentieth time. "What can have happened to them? They have been gone for such a long time."

"It seems long," replied Violet, "but I don't think it's really long. Shall I go out and look for them? The well is at the side of the house, so we can't see it from any of the windows."

"Let's all go," suggested Stella.

"That's a good idea," said Rose. "It's very windy, but it isn't raining. It will do the babies good to have a blow. We'll put on our coats."

The children were overjoyed at the thought of some diversion, and there was much talk of paddling as they dressed.

"It's much too rough, I think," said Rose. "Come to the window and look at the waves. But it will be fun down on the beach."

They were soon ready, and the moment the door was opened they made a dash outside. But none of them were prepared for the strength of the gale that was blowing, and for a moment they clung together, hardly able to stand against it.

"I never thought it would be so rough as this," gasped Rose. "We'll only go a little way, just to meet the boys."

"My cap, my cap!" shrieked Maurice, as the wind took it and whirled it away high in the air. The children gazed after it helplessly, while Maurice clutched his head and howled.

"It's gone!" cried Rose. "We can never catch it now. Come in again."

She and Violet dragged the babies back into the

cottage, all very breathless and disheveled. and Maurice still crying lustily for his cap.

"Never mind, Maurice," Rose comforted. "It's very nice to go without a hat. Your hair will grow ever so thick and curly. Just fancy the wind being so strong!"

"Did you see the boys?" inquired Violet.

"I forgot to look for them," confessed Rose, "but I expect they'll turn up soon. No wonder it takes them such an age to get to the well and back when it's so rough. I know what we'll do now. We'll all look in the cupboard and see what we can find for lunch."

Maurice stopped crying, and joined in the cheer that hailed this popular suggestion. Off went hats and coats, and the children gathered round Rose.

"We'll turn everything out," she said. "I'll stand by the cupboard and hand the things out to Stella, Stella can pass them to Anthony, and Anthony can pass them to Maurice, and Maurice can pass them to Violet, and Violet can put them on the table."

So half an hour later, when Charles burst into the room, the table was piled with tins and bags of every description, and the children were flushed and excited.

"Oh, boys!" began Rose. Then she saw only Charles' terrified face, as he stood gasping for breath just inside the door. "Charles," she cried, "what ever is the matter? Where's William?"

"William—William——" he panted, and stopped, looking at Rose with frightened eyes.

"Where's William?" she almost screamed, rushing at him, and seizing him by the arm.

"In the well," he said, with something very near a sob. "Oh, Rose! I tried to get him out, and I can't."

"Is he dead?" she asked in a far-away voice that did not sound in the least like her own.

"No, he's not dead. But I can't get him out. I tried and I tried—but I can't!"

"I'll come and help," said Rose. "Can't he climb out?"

"The chain isn't safe. It broke, and I only just managed to catch the end. I fastened it round the post again, but I'm afraid it will break again—and then William will be drowned."

"Here's a piece of rope. There's a lot of it in the bottom of the cupboard. Now then, quick!"

Charles took the rope, and fled out of the cottage. Rose flew after him, and the rest of the Seven followed. In their panic they forgot the storm. As they struggled against it, fighting their way to the well, their only thought was of William.

Charles got there first. He lay flat and shouted down:

"William, William! I've got a rope. Hold on a bit longer, while I make it fast to the post."

"Don't hurry," came a hollow voice from the depths. "Be sure you tie a reefer knot."

Rose was now lying by Charles' side, and could see William's face shining palely through the gloom.

"Look out, Rose!" he shouted up to her, "don't *you* fall in."

"Rather not!" she answered. Then she scrambled quickly to her feet as she heard a warning cry from Charles, and was just in time to stop the babies' attempts to look down the well.

"Come and see Charles tie a reefer knot," she said. "And then if you stand still by this post you'll see William come up out of the well like a Jack-in-the-box."

They all squatted round the post, and watched Charles with great interest while he deftly made one end of the rope fast and prepared to throw the other down to William.

"Are you absolutely sure it's safe?" cried Rose. "Let's try it first. Here, you children, stand away in a line, and all pull on it together, just as you do when we have a tug-of-war."

So the knot was tested, and found to be immovable, and then the end was dropped down the well.

"It's quite firm, William," cried Charles. "Can you climb up, or shall we pull you?"

"I think I can climb up, once I get started. It's difficult because my boots are so wet. They slip."

After many painful efforts William began steadily to mount. Charles cheered him on, and executed a war dance in his excitement.

"Stand back!" cried Rose, holding on to the end of his coat.

"It's all right!" he yelled. "He's coming!"

It was true. In another moment they saw William's head appearing out of the well.

"How can I get out?" he gasped.

"Hold tight," shouted Charles, "and we'll give you a hand. Hold me round the waist, Rose, and Violet, you hold Rose, and all you others hang on, and I'll be able to give him a pull."

With much shouting and manœuvring the living chain was formed.

"Now," said Charles at last, "when I say 'pull,' all stand firm and pull."

He stood at the edge of the well, and bent down and caught hold of William behind the shoulders, under the arms.

"Hold on to the rope, and put your hands on the edge, William. And, when I say 'pull' to the others, you give a heave up."

All worked perfectly according to plan. Charles cried "pull," William gave a gigantic heave up, the children held on to each other and pulled with all their might, and the next thing they knew they were all lying on their backs, with William floundering about on top of them. They picked themselves and each other up, and Charles put his arm through William's.

"Come on!" he said, "let's run home."

"The water!" cried Rose. "We haven't got any water yet."

"Oh, bother the water!" exclaimed Charles.

"I'm all right," gasped the dripping William, who was now shaking all over after his fright and his wetting. "Come on, Charles, we'll get it now, we don't want to come back here again today."

"You go home, William," interrupted Rose,

"Charles and I can get it. You must take off those wet things."

"Yes, go on, old chap," said Charles, letting go his arm, and giving him a push. "And take the babies with you. Now, you babies, run a race with William!"

They flew off, almost blown along by the wind, and when Rose and Charles staggered into the cottage a few minutes later, triumphantly carrying a bucket that was nearly full, they were met by William gracefully draped in a rug. His teeth were still chattering with cold, and he looked pale and hollow-eyed.

"I challenge you to a wrestling match," cried Charles, dumping down the bucket. "That's the stuff to warm you up. I bet you won't lay me out."

"Go into the front room, then," said Rose, who knew what their wrestling matches were like. "We don't all want to be laid out."

They ran off, and a tremendous racket arose in the cottage. A stranger entering it would have thought that some local earthquake was in motion. The walls shook and the door rattled violently as the boys rushed, and scuffled, and bumped about. When they reappeared, both were flushed and breathless, but

William's teeth no longer chattered, and his face wore his usual broad smile.

"Now we'll cook lunch," he said.

Lunch turned out to be very much like breakfast, only that instead of kippers the Seven had sardines. They had found a tin of ship's biscuits in the store cupboard, which they all took for dog biscuits, but, as Charles said, when you are hungry, any kind of biscuits are delicious and, somehow, dog biscuits were better than plain dog, on which many polar explorers had had to live for weeks at a time.

"I expect they left dog biscuits here instead of the ordinary kind because they keep better," said Rose, as she sat munching her portion.

"I should think it's because there's more nourishment in them," mumbled Charles, with his mouth full. "Just fancy giving shipwrecked sailors cracknels, or chocolate wafers! Why, I could eat a whole tin of them straight off myself, and I bet a shipwrecked sailor could eat six."

"I'm jolly glad there are none washed up here now," said William. "There'd never be enough food to go round for more than a day or two. I wonder how those six French sailors that Robert told us about, managed to live here for six weeks."

"I know, I know!" cried Charles excitedly, getting up from his stool and capering round the table. "Don't you remember? Rabbits! Robert said there were millions of rabbits. We'll go and catch some at once. Hurry up, William."

William jumped up, stuffing the remainder of his biscuit in his pocket; but suddenly Rose got up and stood between them and the door.

"No, you won't, boys," she said emphatically. "You were the whole morning getting a bucket of water and falling down the well. If you go out now catching rabbits I know you'll be the whole afternoon catching each other, or getting caught in the traps, and I'm not going to be left alone again to look after the babies."

"Hear, hear!" agreed Violet and Stella, while the babies clamored to go out with the boys.

"But we must have food," protested Charles.

"Yes, we must," said Rose. "You said that this morning, and you were going to cook lunch, and sort out the stores in the cupboard."

"I opened the tin of sardines, and we've had a jolly good lunch," said Charles.

"It was very nice," Rose admitted, "but we haven't eaten much. In half an hour we shall all be starving again, and the babies will start howling and be as cross as two sticks."

"We must catch rabbits before we can cook them," put in William.

"And men always do the hunting," added Charles, "and women do the cooking and look after the babies. So it's quite fair."

Rose's eyes filled with tears. She was tired out with the strain of the morning, and perhaps more than any of the others she missed her mother, and her mother's happy courage in dealing with worries and difficulties. Violet saw how near she was to the breaking-point, and stepped gallantly in to take up the cudgels for her.

"It's not fair at all," she cried, with some heat. "We looked after the babies all the morning, and you did nothing. Men don't play about, and fall down wells, and have to be rescued."

"We didn't play about," contradicted William indignantly. "The wind blew me down the well. I couldn't help it."

"Poor little boy—got blown down the well" mocked Stella.

"If you start quarreling we shan't get any rabbits, or tea, or anything else," said Charles.

The babies set up a wail, and cried that they wanted to go out and catch rabbits. They had caught the spirit of dissension that had arisen among the elders, and they refused to obey Rose when she told them to sit still at table till they had finished their biscuit. For a few minutes the children pushed and jostled one another angrily, and there was a babel of cries in the room.

"Charles, Charles," cried Rose, "do try to stop them. They will hurt each other. Oh, if only Mother would come!"

Charles, who at that moment was trying to hold a kicking, struggling Maurice down on his chair by dint of considerable force, suddenly let go his grip of the child and stood looking at Rose's appealing face. Coming at such a moment the thought of the mother he loved so dearly struck him almost like a physical blow. He seemed to see her reproachful eyes looking at him, and to hear her soft, reproving "Oh, Charles!" Maurice had ceased his cries in the astonishment of feeling himself so quickly released, and now sat quite quiet, looking up at his brother with solemn round eyes, his face wet with tears. The other children turned from their squabbling, their attention caught by the suddenness of the change from angry howls to silence, and there was a moment's quiet among them.

Seized by some quick inspiration Charles jumped on a stool, and stood with his hand raised to address the crowd.

"Friends, Countrymen, Islanders," he began, "listen to me. If we fight each other, we shall turn into savages."

"Hear, hear!" put in William.

"We have been here a day and a night," continued Charles, thrusting aside a strong desire to punch his brother's head. "Think of the number of days and nights, we shall be here if we stay for six weeks!"

"Forty-two," said Stella promptly.

"Now divide by a hundred and subtract six," murmured William.

"When explorers find a continent or an island," continued the orator, ignoring the interruptions, "they take possession of it and plant their flag. Then they appoint a ruler and make laws, so that the people can get on with their work in peace, instead of fighting."

"I'd much rather fight than work," said William.

"If everyone fought, no one would have anything to eat," said Rose.

"The first thing to do now," said Charles, "is to appoint a chieftain."

"That's a sensible idea," agreed William. "Shall we draw lots?"

"I think that we three eldest ones must take it in turns, don't you, Rose?"

"Yes. We could take it in turns—one day each."

"That's the stuff," said William. "Who shall be first?"

"I think Rose ought to take it on today," said Charles, after a moment's reflection. "She did do most of the work this morning," he added generously.

"Then we certainly shan't go rabbiting today," sighed William regretfully. "But what a lovely day we'll have when *I* am Chief!"

"Have I begun to rule yet?" asked Rose eagerly.

"Rather!" cried the boys. "Fire away."

"I think you ought to wear a crown—or feathers in your hair, like a real Chief," said Stella. "We might forget who you are, Rose."

"I've got a brooch," cried Violet. "Shall I lend it to you? If the Chief always wears it, we shan't get mixed up."

"That's a good idea," said Charles. "Put it on

Rose. Now then everybody, attend! Our Chief is about to speak."

"First, wash up," cried Rose in a commanding voice. "Next, sort out the stores and pack them back so that we know where they all are, and how much we've got."

"Right ho, Miss—I mean Your Majesty," cried William, and the elder ones started with enthusiasm to obey the orders of their Chief, while the younger ones rushed about and got in the way in their efforts to be of service. They soon had the plates stacked up in a neat pile, all spotlessly clean, and then began the real business of the afternoon.

"We must make a list of all that we have—like Robinson Crusoe," said Charles. "What a good thing that I had my pencil in my pocket!"

He carefully tore off the margin from one of the newspapers on which to make his list.

"There's a notice pinned up here to say that there's some oil in a drum outside the house," said Rose, going to the cupboard. "Directly we have finished sorting out the stores, see if the stove has oil in it, and if not, fill it up from the drum."

"Don't you think we ought to do that first, Rose, before it gets dark?" suggested William.

"No, certainly not," said Rose emphatically. She knew the boys too well to be put off the path she had mapped out by any red herring they tried to draw across it. She was thoroughly enjoying the powers of her high position. Never before had her brothers obeyed her, and she felt that she must make the most of this golden opportunity.

"What happens to chieftains who turn into tyrants, Charles?" asked William, with a tremendous wink at his brother.

"They die an early death," said Charles solemnly, "torn in pieces by any angry populace."

"There, Rose, let those words be a warning to you. History repeats itself."

Rose laughed good humoredly. "All right," she said, "but anyhow, by then the store-cupboard will be in good order. Now, Charles, you be ready to write out the list while we call the things out to you."

For the next half-hour there was continuous counting, and sorting, and recounting. The babies insisted on helping, and to keep them quiet they were allowed to do pretty much as they pleased, which very much lengthened the proceedings. But at last the work was completed to the satisfaction of everyone, the

store-cupboard was in apple-pie order, and this was
the list that Charles read out to them:

```
17 tins of sardines
23 tins of fish (all sorts)
12 tins of pressed beef
24 tins of fruit (mostly pineapple chunks)
12 tins of milk
 1 tin of biscuits
 1 tin of tea
 1 bag of flour
 1 bag of oatmeal
 1 bag of brown sugar
 1 bag of rice
 1 sack of potatoes
 1 large pot of jam (plum and apple)
 1 packet of candles
 1 packet of matches
 2 slabs of soap.
```

"Well, that's done," he finished off with a sigh of
relief. It had been a long job, and toward the end
of it all the children were tired. They would have
slacked off and left it, but the Chieftain was adamant,
and would allow no sidetracking from their set task.

"And I think it's a jolly useful lot of stuff," said
William. "A good thing too, because I feel starving.
What about tea? We might have some more
sardines."

"No, we've had enough fish for today," decided
Rose. "I think we ought to have biscuits and jam,

and some tea to drink. We might open one of the tins of milk. See to the stove, boys, and boil the kettle."

"I vote we eat something first, and make tea afterwards," suggested William. "It will take ages to get the stove in working order, and ages more for that kettle to boil. I can't wait or I shall be too weak to eat. That's what happens to people who go too long without food. It hurts at first, but then they get so that they can't bear the sight of a meal."

"It would be a long time before *you* got to that stage," said Charles.

"Oh, Rose, high and mighty Chief, let's have something to eat," implored William, ignoring Charles' remark, and the babies lustily supported his prayer. Rose, who was feeling very hungry herself, was pleased graciously to grant their request.

"Lay tea," she commanded.

"And don't cut the bread too thin, nor spread the butter too thick," added William.

Tony

CHAPTER XI

A SURPRISE FROM THE BLUE

CHARLES was the first to wake the next morning, and almost before his eyes were open he had jumped up from his sleeping place and was shaking William vigorously by the shoulder.

"Wake up!" he cried, "and let's see who's to be Chief today."

William gave a sleepy grunt; then, as the pleasant prospect of the day dawned on him, he too sprang to his feet.

"Why not go on upwards?" he said. "Rose first, me next, and you last because you're the eldest."

"No, we said yesterday that we'd draw lots.   So come along."

Without stopping to put on their coats they ran downstairs. From one of the newspapers they tore off two slips and, after much careful measurement, folded them and placed them both in a hat belonging to one of the girls.

"Now close your eyes and take one," said Charles, shaking the hat with great energy. "The longest one for the Chief!"

William shut his eyes tight and turned away his head, then picked a slip from the hat held out to him. It was the longest.

"Hurrah!" he shouted triumphantly. "I said I ought to be Chief and that shows I was right. What a gorgeous day we're going to have!"

Charles looked disappointed. As eldest he was used to taking the lead in all their activities, and he did not like the prospect of being ordered about by his young brother. But he bowed to Fate with as good a grace as he could muster, and snapped out a curt "all right."

"It will be your turn tomorrow," comforted William. Then after a moment's pause he added, "You can have it today if you like—I don't mind."

"No, we drew lots and you won," said Charles decidedly. "Come along and get your brooch." William's generous offer had completely restored his good humor and, in refusing it, his feeling of jealousy disappeared, and he entered fully into the spirit of the pact.

When they got downstairs again the rest of the Seven were completing their scanty toilet.

"We can't wash," complained Rose. "There's no water."

"The brooch, the brooch!" shouted William. Then as he fastened it on his shirt he turned to Charles.

"Hasten, slave, and hie thee to the well to draw water," he commanded.

"Don't be an ass," retorted his brother, as they linked arms and went tramping down the stairs together, followed by a parting warning from Stella not to be naughty little boys and play with the water.

"You wait till I come back!" said the Chief, as they went out, banging the door behind them.

The gale had abated a little; but the morning was gray, and wild with the roar of the sea.

"A good job it's not raining," said Charles, as they set out at a run, "just look at that spray coming over the rocks! No one will be able to come for us today."

"I should jolly well hope they won't! I want to be Chief, and go rabbiting."

"So do I. But I should like some fried bacon for breakfast. I feel weak."

"I don't believe there's much *goodness* in sardines," sighed William, rather downcast at the thought of the fried bacon so far beyond their reach.

They got the water and returned to the cottage without misadventure, to find breakfast all ready. Rose had opened another tin of sardines. The boys looked at one another and groaned heavily.

"We ought to make some porridge today, ready for tomorrow morning," remarked Rose brightly. "It will be a change."

"Couldn't we have some for lunch?" asked William plaintively. Then he suddenly realized the powers conferred on him by his exalted position, and his voice changed to one of command.

"We'll have porridge for lunch," he said. "Hot, with heaps of sugar."

"Good for you, William," encouraged his brother. "Can't you order a fruit salad too, or a suet pudding and treacle?"

"Don't, Charles," implored Rose. "I can't bear to think of it. Perhaps it will get calm today, and then Daddy will come for us."

She looked longingly out of the window, and the babies began excitedly to talk of going home and of treacle puddings.

"It won't get calm today," interrupted Charles decidedly. "The sea is as rough as ever, though it's not so windy."

"Never mind," comforted William, as the joyous anticipations of the younger children turned to disappointed cries. "You shall all come out with me and catch rabbits."

"We must make some traps directly after breakfast," said Charles. "There's plenty of string. And I don't expect——"

"What ever's that?" interrupted Rose, sharply. She had been gazing disconsolately out of the window, and now ran to it, pointing upwards at the sky.

"An aeroplane, an aeroplane!" shouted all the children.

"Fancy an aeroplane coming over here," said Charles. "I wonder where it's going!"

"It's coming this way!" cried the Chief. "Let's go out and have a look at it."

In another moment they were all rushing out of the door; but Rose held Charles back by the arm.

"Charles—can it be Daddy—coming to fetch us?" she whispered.

Charles shook his head. Then he stared at the fast-approaching machine, and a wave of hope swept through him.

"It's coming straight for us," he cried. "I bet it *is* Daddy. Oh, Rose, how lovely! Come along, let's go outside."

He joined the others, with whoops of joy.

"I bet it's Daddy," he shouted, now quite convinced of it. "Come along down to the sands."

The aeroplane suddenly swerved and swooped downwards, describing great circles almost directly above their heads. No sound of its engine came to them through the noise of the breakers on the rocks all round them, and they grew silent with awe as they watched this strange, eerie, bird-like thing which, in its turn, they felt was watching them. They could see in it small black objects that they guessed were men, but they were not near enough to recognize any one form, strain their eyes as they might. Then the wonderful vision flew upwards and away from them and across the island, and there was a sob of disappointment; but, before they could speak, it was flying back again, and circling round the shores.

"It can't land—it's looking for a flat place!" cried Charles, in an agony of suspense.

"And there's nothing but rocks—rocks on the island, and rocks in the sea, and rocks everywhere," groaned William, quite forgetting the delights of chieftainship in his excitement.

"I wish they would come lower so that we could see them," said Violet.

"Look, look!" cried Rose. "What ever are they going to do now?"

The great machine was hovering in the air, and as they gazed at it they saw a black object fall from it right on to the sands.

"It's Daddy, it's Daddy!" shrieked Stella. "He's jumped out!"

Heedless of the roughness of the ground they all made their way helter-skelter, as fast as they could scramble along, to the crumpled heap lying on the sands.

"It's a sack," cried Charles, as he reached it, neck and neck with William.

"And here's an envelope tied on to it. It has *Open*

at once printed on it. Quick, Charles, see what's in it."

They pulled the envelope off the string, and tore it open. Inside was a typewritten letter.

"It's from Daddy and Mummy, I'm sure. Read it out loud," cried Rose, who had come up with the rest of the Seven.

"I'm glad it's typewritten," said Charles. "Listen!"

He knelt down, and sheltered the sheet of paper from the wind behind a large stone, then read:

Dear Children,
    We tried to come to you in the boat, but it was too rough. We want to know if you are all safe and well. If you are, will you all stand outside the house in a row, so that we can count you, and wave your hands? If any of you are ill or in trouble you must all go into the house except one, and let one alone stand outside and wave. There is some food in the bag. We expect you have found the food in the house, and the water in the well, as Robert told you all about them. We know you are brave, and we hope you are happy. We will come to you the instant we are able. In three days' time, if it is still too rough for a boat, we will come by aeroplane and drop another parcel. The aeroplane cannot land because the ground is too rocky.
                                    Your loving DADDY and MUMMY.

"Hurrah, hurrah! It's Daddy and Mummy!" shouted the Seven, dancing about in their excitement, and waving wildly to the hovering aeroplane.

"Get in a row, quick!" cried William. "Stand in a straight line, and then all shout at once, and wave."

The children arranged themselves in order, and a loud yell arose from them, while they jumped wildly up and down and waved. The great bird-like machine circled for a minute or more above their heads, then made off quickly on the way it had come, watched out of sight by the still waving Seven.

"Oh, what fun!" cried Charles, sinking down for a moment exhausted on the ground.

"How lovely of them to come!" panted Rose. "Do you think they were really there?"

"Of course they were," said Charles. "They said so in their letter."

"Read it again," implored Rose.

So Charles read the letter through again.

"Now let's see what's in the bag," he cried, jumping up.

"Shall we take it indoors, and unpack it there?" suggested Rose.

"Carry the bag indoors, Charles," said the Chief in a loud, commanding voice, coming back to the glories of his high position.

Never was parcel unpacked with more delight than the one that had reached the Seven so dramatically. One by one the various packets were drawn forth, and wild cries of pleasure greeted each fresh delicacy that was unfolded. First there was some home-made brawn in a basin, two big cakes, and a pot of butter. Then came a bag of apples and a box of figs. Perhaps the find that received the greatest welcome was six large loaves of bread.

"What wonderful loaves!" cried Rose. "Doesn't the crust look a lovely color?"

"I feel terribly hungry," said Charles, with a meaning look at the Chief.

William rose to the suggestion. "I command everyone who would like a slice of dry bread to sit down," he said in a decisive voice.

There was a loud thump on the floor—all dropped on to it as one man. William got a knife and with great ceremony cut one of the loaves into seven large hunks.

"We must take the first bite all together at the same time," he said. "I will count, 'One, two, three,' and when I say 'three' you may begin."

"It sounds like a race," said Charles. "The babies always choke if they eat too fast."

"It *is* a race; but it's a slow race. The one who finishes his slice the last will win," announced the

Chief with quick resource. "Now then, ready! One, two, three——"

"I've never tasted such wonderful bread before," said Charles, breaking a short spell of silence. "I wonder you don't write a poem about it, William."

William went on munching steadily for a second or two, but he could not resist the call of so unparalleled an invitation, and rising to his feet and standing with his hand on his heart, he uttered these lines:

> "O staff of life,
> How sweet thou art!
> I love thee more
> Than apple tart!"

Loud and undivided applause from the Six greeted this poetic tribute.

"Go on, William," cried Violet encouragingly, "do say another verse."

"Yes, another verse please," cried Charles, rapping the floor with a spoon that lay handy by way of encouragement.

"No," said the Chieftain grimly, "I'm too hungry." He sat down and once more the Seven ate in silence. Rose won the slow race by one mouthful.

"Now for the rabbit hunt," said William. "Get the string ready and we'll make those traps."

"What about porridge for lunch?" asked Rose.

"I think you worry too much about food," replied William, now feeling a pleasant tightness under his belt. "Exercise is what we need, so I vote—I mean I decree—that we set our traps, and then explore the island a bit."

"Can't we go for a picnic?" cried Violet.

"It's too rough," said Rose. "I don't believe we could find a sheltered spot in the whole place."

"No, I'm sure there isn't one," agreed Charles. "But we might put an apple each in our pockets, to eat as we go along, and come home again about tea-time. We don't want to waste a whole day just hanging about, cooking food and that sort of thing—do we, William?"

"Certainly not, Charles. How many apples are there?"

"There are forty-five," said Rose. "I counted them when we took them out of the bag."

William pondered for a few moments, with puckered brows.

"That is two each for three days, and three over," he announced at length. "They must be made to last till the aeroplane comes again."

"Good little boy!" interrupted Stella, cheekily. "You really ought to go up top."

"Take one each," went on the Chief with a withering look at his sister. "Put it in your pocket. Get your coats on ready to set out—and then play about a bit till Charles and I have made the traps."

"We haven't washed yet," Rose reminded him.

"There's plenty of water if you really want a wash. I'm clean, so I don't need one. I think it would be a waste of water, don't you, Charles?"

Charles heartily agreed. The last thing the boys wanted at that moment was another journey to the well. And at no time did they believe in washing for its own sake.

"If you really want a job, Rose, why not make the porridge, as you have talked so much about it?" said Charles. "And after that you might divide up the loaves and things into three portions, so that we shall have something jolly to eat every day, till the next delivery comes. Don't you think that would be a good plan, William?"

"An excellent plan, Charles. Proceed with the work, Rose. The babies can help you. Then perhaps we shall have some peace, and be able to get on with our traps. Maurice is getting everything tied up into knots."

"No, I'm not," contradicted Maurice, struggling violently against his forcible removal to the other side of the room.

"I know what," cooed William in the honeyed tones the boys adopted when trying to persuade the younger ones to do something they didn't want to do. "You help Rose stir the porridge, and perhaps she will let you taste it."

"I don't want to stir porridge. I want to make traps."

"Give him a bit of string, William, and let him mess about by himself," suggested Charles.

By dint of bribery, tactful persuasion, and a certain amount of force, combined, the peace was kept, the porridge was cooked, and six traps were made ready to set. By this time the morning was well advanced, and when Stella suggested lunch before setting out on their picnic, there was hearty cry of approval from all but William. He groaned—he thought it due to his chieftainship—and warned them that if they did nothing but eat they would never achieve any success in life.

"You will grow worse than savages," he declared. "Why, even in the Stone Age, people carved and painted and made pottery, while all you do is to eat one meal, and then think of the next."

"Well, William, why don't you go along and do a bit of carving?" suggested Rose kindly. "There are sure to be plenty of caves among the rocks that want decorating. We'll see to the babies, and have lunch, and come and look for you later on."

"We've got those traps to set," objected William. "Hurry up and eat if you must."

"What shall we have?"

"There's the porridge," suggested Rose.

"That will keep till tomorrow morning," interrupted William, waking up to a sudden interest in the meal. "We'll have brawn, and bread, and a tin of pineapple chunks. Plates, Charles, and be quick."

"Six plates?" asked Charles, with a sly wink at Rose.

"No, seven," said the Chief firmly.

CHAPTER XII

THE THIRD CAVE

WHEN the Seven set out from the cottage the sun was shining fitfully through scudding clouds.

"I do believe it's going to clear up," said Rose. "I wish this wind would stop blowing."

"Rose, you take the babies along to the end of the island while Charles and I set the traps," ordered William. "I expect you'll find a cave there, and you can mess about in that till we come. Come along, Charles—we'll go to the hollow beyond the well. I'll race you there."

No sooner said than done. Without waiting a moment, off scampered both boys, leaving the rest gazing disconsolately after them.

"Boys, boys," screamed Rose, "I want you!" But the sound of her voice was blown away on the wind, and the boys continued their helter-skelter rush toward the well.

"Now what are we to do?" she asked Stella, who had joined in the vain hallooing. "They won't know where we are, and they will never be able to meet us."

"William said we were to go to the end of the island and look for a cave," suggested Violet, while Anthony and Maurice began to clamor for a cave and a game of smugglers.

"Can't you see that the island is *all* 'end'?" said Rose in tones of deep dejection. "I don't even know where it begins."

"Don't let's bother about the boys," put in Stella. "It's all their fault anyhow, and if they can't find us they can look for us. I vote we go straight on, and if we don't find a cave there we can come home again."

This seemed a sensible plan, and they proceeded to carry it out because no one could think of any other. Almost unconsciously they took the way of least resistance to the wind, and were soon running gleefully before it. In less time than seemed possible they came to a line of shore, with rocks jutting far out, over which the waves were breaking in great sheets of sea and spray.

"There might be a cave round that corner," said Rose, pointing to a place where the land ended in low cliffs of rock. "We shan't be able to paddle, but we can easily walk over the rocks."

The children were always ready for any adventure, and in next to no time they were jumping from rock to rock, the babies being dragged along by their elders amid exclamations of delight mingled with squeals of pretended horror, as one or the other slipped into some shallow pool that lay between the boulders. By the time they had gone a hundred yards they were all frankly wading, and soaked to well above their waists.

"It's no use bothering about getting our shoes wet," Rose had decided. "We can very soon dry them in this wind on our way home. Oh, isn't it wonderful!"

This last exclamation was called forth by the scene before them as they got round the big rock that had hidden the next bit of shore from their view. For there they came suddenly upon a narrow cove, running some way inland, and finishing in low, straight cliffs. Between them and the cliffs the line of rock on which they stood ended, and gave place to a tiny beach of fine shingle. And in the cliffs were the round black openings of three caves.

The children had hoped to find *one* cave. To see *three,* all in a row, was greater joy than they had

They peered half fearfully into the cave.

ever imagined. Scrambling, shouting, now hitting
up rocks, now floundering in water, the Fire-scouts
reached the shingle beach, and were peering half-
fearfully into the mouth of the first cave. The wind
still whistled above, and around them, but in this
narrow bay they were sheltered.

"Do you think there are any smugglers inside?"
asked Tom.

"Perhaps bears live in there!" said whispered
Maurice.

"There aren't any smugglers or bears left anywhere
near here to-day," said Dick, scornfully. "They've
all been killed long ago."

"Then why don't you go in and explore?" suggested Violet.

"I think so; so empty," interposed Ron, forcing
his way into a long battle of words, if nothing worse, between his two uncles. "We'll all go in together.
I wish I didn't look so dark inside. Let's give a
good shout first!"

Their voices went echoing round the cave, and
died away in faint murmurings among the cliffs of
the little cove. Again and again they shouted, and
listened to the quick-following clamor, that sent the
sea-gulls flying round them, screaming in protest

ever imagined. Scrambling, shouting, now toiling up rocks, now floundering in water, the Five soon reached the shingle beach, and were peering half-fearfully into the mouth of the first cave. The wind still whistled above and around them, but in this narrow bay they were sheltered.

"Do you think there are any smugglers inside?" asked Tony.

"Perhaps bears live in there!" half whispered Maurice.

"There aren't any smugglers or bears left anywhere near here, sillies," said Stella scornfully. "They've all been killed long ago."

"Then why don't you go in and explore?" suggested Violet.

"I think they're empty," interposed Rose, foreseeing a long battle of words, if nothing worse, between her two juniors. "We'll all go in together. I wish it didn't look so dark inside. Let's give a good shout first."

Their voices went echoing round the cave, and died away in faint murmurings among the cliffs of the little cove. Again and again they shouted, and listened to the quick following clamor, that sent all the seagulls flying round them, screaming in protest at the invasion of their fastness by these noisy human creatures. But from the cave came no sign of life. Little by little the children gathered courage, and ventured farther and farther into its depths. As their eyes became used to the dim light they saw only a large circular chamber, whose dark shadowy walls came smoothly down to its shingle floor.

"It's quite a nice cave," said Rose at length, in disappointed tones, "but no smuggler could hide in it. Come along, and see what the next one is like."

The children rushed out, beguiled by the lure of the unknown, and dived into the darkness of the second cave. Having found nothing alarming in one cave their fears had all vanished, and they now vied with each other in being first to make some new and startling discovery.

The second cave was larger than the first; but its shape was as evenly circular, and its walls as smooth and unbroken. It held no promise of any hiding-place for fabled smugglers or bears.

"There's still one more," said Rose hopefully. "That will be the third, and there's always something wonderful about the third."

The children responded by making a wild dash for the magical third, and as they entered it Rose

gave a whoop of joy. She had been right. It was
the most wonderful cave of all. For there, in the
middle of its farthest end, a small black hole loomed
from the surrounding shadows. Without a doubt it
was the entrance to some secret passage!

"I wonder where it goes?" exclaimed Violet. "It's
rather low, but I expect we could squeeze through."

"It's just like the hole that Alice in Wonderland
went down," shouted Stella, dancing about gleefully.
"What ever do you think we shall find at the end
of it?"

"I wish we could find the Mad Hatter," said
Violet. "He might ask us to a tea party. Do you
think we ought to wait for the boys?"

"It's no good waiting for them now," said Rose.
"They won't know a bit which way we've gone, and
I don't believe they'll ever find us. We'll explore
the passage a little way, and then it will be time to
go home. Oh, I do hope we find a real smugglers'
cave! Won't it be fun to tell the boys if we
do!"

"Rather!" shouted the others. "Do come on
quickly. Who's going first?"

After a good deal of discussion it was decided that
Stella should lead the way, as she was the thinnest

of the elders, then Violet, followed by the babies, with Rose bringing up the rear.

"If the hole gets very small be sure you don't go on and get stuck," instructed Rose, suddenly feeling the weight of her responsibility as the eldest in charge. "And be sure you feel the ground in front of you with your hands before you crawl on to it, in case you come to a bottomless pit or a well that goes to the sea. And keep on shouting all the time to tell us if it's all right."

Stella promised to carry out all these orders, and the Five knelt down in line, ready to start on their voyage of discovery.

"We shall look just like a train going through a tunnel," exclaimed Violet.

"Here goes the engine! *Puff, puff, puff!*" snorted Stella, crawling forward and disappearing slowly into the blackness of the opening.

Violet followed close on her heels, and gradually the whole train of children was engulfed, till only the soles of a pair of old sand-shoes, the last bit of Rose, were visible. Then they too faded from view, and the cave was once more in silent shadowy darkness, with no sign of life save where the damp shingle of its floor had been disturbed by the tread of many small feet.

Outside in the cove the seagulls again circled and cried to one another in fierce glee, and out on the rocks the sea came wildly dashing. The boulders over which the children had so lately passed were fast becoming wholly submerged, and every wave seemed to break nearer than the last to the little shingle beach.

Meanwhile the boys had not been idle. When they had finished setting the traps to their complete satisfaction the sun had traveled a considerable way on its path to the west.

"I wonder what Robert would think of these traps," said Charles. "I think they're pretty good. I expect we'll get no end of rabbits by the morning."

"What shall we do with them all?" asked William anxiously. "I don't suppose we could eat more than three or four for lunch. Do you think they'll keep?"

"Oh, yes, they keep for ages if they're in a cool place. We might hang some up outside somewhere in the wind. Rabbit-pie is lovely. Do you remember the one Matilda made?"

"Rather! I saw her make it, too. It's quite easy. You just cut them up, and then mix some flour with a drop of water till it looks like putty, and spread it over the top. We haven't got a dish, but I expect it would turn out just as well in an old tin."

"I wish it was cooked now," said Charles. "I feel awfully hungry."

"Well, let's eat our apples. And then I suppose we'd better look for the kids."

"All right," agreed Charles. "I wonder where all the rabbits are," he continued musingly, as they sat down on a stone and began slowly to munch. "We haven't seen one yet. Do *you* think it's cruel to kill them?"

"Robert doesn't, you know. He says it's a kindness really, because the rest get more grass to eat. He doesn't think they'll ever die out, or have to be preserved, because there are such crowds of them. In Australia he says there are several millions and they have grown so fierce that they often attack the natives and kill them."

"Do you think they do?" asked Charles, looking grave but a trifle skeptical. "I believe Robert made that up. Did he say he'd been to Australia?"

"No, but he's got a nephew out there, and he wrote and told him about it. He said you could hear the natives shrieking for miles, and all the Englishmen out there have to be special constables."

"I believe his nephew was pulling his leg. No one could be frightened of a rabbit. I wouldn't mind if I met a million."

"Would you rather meet a million rabbits or one lion?" asked William.

"A million rabbits, of course, which would you?"

"I think a million rabbits, too."

"Well, come on now, and find the others," said Charles, jumping up. "Which way did they go?"

"I told them to go to the end of the island," said William.

"Which way is that?"

"Why, over there, of course," said William decidedly, pointing in the opposite direction to that taken by the Five. "Let's have a race."

For the next two hours the boys rushed about from end to end of the island, till they had scoured every inch of rising ground, and scanned the whole shore for some sign of the rest of the family. At first they frolicked about light-heartedly, but, as they grew tired and realized the difficulty of the task they had set themselves, they began to get cross, and then anxious.

"Perhaps they have gone home," suggested William at last. "Rose must know it's getting late."

"But you told her to wait for us, and as you're Chief today perhaps she thought she ought to obey you."

"She might have known I never meant her to wait

all night," said William crossly. "We said we would go home for tea."

"Well, come along to the cottage. I expect they are waiting there for us."

With hopes rising high they made straight for home. But inside the cottage all was silent, and they both felt a chill of fear as they looked eagerly into each empty room.

"What shall we do now?" asked William, as they came back into the kitchen.

"I suppose we'd better go and have another good hunt," replied Charles. "You go one way and I'll go the other, and one of us is sure to see them somewhere."

"All right," agreed his brother dejectedly. "What shall we do if we find them?"

"Bring them straight home and get tea. If we don't meet each other halfway round it will show that one of us has met them."

They separated and went off at a run for, tired as they were, they felt that the children must be found, and found quickly, and the growing fear of accidents that might have befallen lent wings to their feet.

When they met, about a quarter of an hour later, they were both hoarse with shouting, and exhausted.

They almost fell into each other's arms and sank down together on the ground with pale faces and frightened eyes.

"It's nearly high tide," said Charles hoarsely. "They must have got caught."

"They never think of tides. We ought to have gone with them. Very soon it will be dark."

At thought of the coming night both boys sprang to their feet and began to run about wildly, calling all the children by name, heedless that the roar of the sea, now dashing high round the island as if its wild fury must engulf it, drowned all other sounds almost as soon as uttered. They kept together now, for neither could face the loneliness of another solitary search.

They peered over the cliffs and rocks; they stood unknowingly above the cave which the children had discovered so short a time before and which now presented a very different scene. Gone were the low rocks over which they had reached it, and gone was the little shingle beach. The sea filled it, the waves sent their foam and spray flying over the low cliffs, the three caves were no longer to be seen. They passed along above other bays and rocky inlets, and at last turned once more to the cottage.

"They may be there by now," half whispered Charles.

"The door is shut and it looks empty," said William, as they drew near. "What shall we do if they aren't there?"

Charles shook his head. He dared not think. They came to the door and opened it slowly, as if loth to have their last hope dispelled. But the silence that met them on the threshold proved beyond doubt that the cottage was as empty as it had looked to William.

"Do you think they're drowned?" asked Charles in a shaky voice.

"They aren't anywhere on the island, or we should have seen them. So they must have been washed away." William leant against the door, and suddenly sobbed. "I wish we were drowned too."

Charles put his arm round his brother.

"Come and have one more look," he said in a voice that he tried hard to make encouraging. "Come on, old chap. We may have missed them somewhere— or they may be hiding, for fun."

With a great effort William pulled himself together, and stumbled blindly away from the cottage by Charles' side to continue the search. Both boys were tired out, and could scarcely set one foot before the other now that they were no longer buoyed up by any hope. They went in silence, broken only by an occasional gasping sob from William.

Suddenly Charles gave a shout and began to run, dragging William with him by the arm.

"Look, look!" he cried. "They're coming—oh, William, quick!"

William looked up and rubbed his sleeve across his eyes, to clear away a mist of tears. In the distance he saw a group of small figures, and as it grew rapidly nearer he saw Stella leading at a quick jog-trot. Close behind her followed Rose and Violet, each dragging one of the babies by the hand. With a wild yell the boys made a sprint forward, and in a few moments were roughly shaking the girls and hugging the babies, as if to assure themselves they were real flesh and blood, and not mere ghosts of their imagination. The returning wanderers were startled into silence by the warmth of a greeting such as they had never expected. Then they all began to talk at once.

"We've found the most wonderful cave in the world," gasped Stella.

"It's got the loveliest passage, with steps all up and down," cried Rose.

"It's all dark," said Maurice.

"I think it's full of bears," said Tony.

"It goes for miles and miles," said Violet. "It's a million times bigger than King Solomon's mines."

"William, what ever is the matter?" asked Rose quickly, as William gave a great sob that would not be repressed. "You look awfully pale. What is it, Charles?"

"He's got a pain inside," explained Charles, holding on to William's arm. "I think he's hungry. We've been waiting for you for ages." He would not for the world have admitted to the girls the anxiety he and William had suffered on their account.

"Oh, dear," cried Rose, "why ever didn't you begin tea? We hurried as much as we could, but the passage was so narrow and long, and the babies couldn't crawl any faster. Come along and have it now. Have you got it ready? Is the pain very bad, William?"

"It is rather," muttered William, as another big sob shook him.

"I'll light the stove at once, and put the kettle on, and give you a cup of hot tea," said the sympathetic

Rose, hurrying toward the cottage. "Perhaps you ought to go to bed at once."

"What he wants is a good solid meal," said Charles gruffly.

Maurice

CHAPTER XIII

TREASURE TROVE

THERE was no doubt about the solidity of the tea to which the Seven presently sat down. The table positively groaned under the weight and variety of the food set out on it. Rose protested faintly that they ought to save for the days to come; but the boys, so recently relieved of their weight of fear, were in no mood for short rations. Their hearts rejoiced, and instinctively they felt the need of a real feast. They opened tins of all sorts with fervor, they set out brawn and cakes and fruit, and they piled all the loaves of bread on the floor within reach because, as Charles said, it was so nice to know they were there.

"How is your pain now, William?" inquired Rose sympathetically, as they sat round the table, helping themselves generously to whatever took their fancy.

"It's getting a bit better," growled William. "Did you get caught by the tide?" he added, by way of turning the conversation to a subject less personal.

"No, did the tide come in? We never noticed it. We found a cave, and crawled through a passage, and——"

"It's miles and miles long!" interrupted Stella.

"Where did it lead then?" asked Charles.

"We came up right in the middle of the island. We saw a light at the end that looked like a star, so we knew it came out somewhere."

"It can't be miles long," objected William, who was fast regaining his usual pugnacity. "The whole island isn't a mile anywhere."

"It seemed miles anyhow," put in Violet. "We had to crawl all the way."

"Why didn't you walk?"

"Because it was so low we couldn't stand up, of course. But we came to an enormous cavern."

"What was it like?" asked Charles, full of eager curiosity.

"We couldn't see. It was too dark," said Rose.

"Then how did you know it was enormous?"

"Because we couldn't feel any sides or top to it. We tried to go round it, only then we couldn't see the light at the end, and we were afraid of losing our way."

"Through caverns measureless to man," murmured William.

"Let's go and look at it after tea, and take a lamp," said Charles, forgetting his tiredness.

"No," said Rose firmly. "It's getting late, and the babies are tired and ought to go to bed."

"Charles and I will go alone," announced William, suddenly bethinking himself of his powers as Chief. "You needn't come with us."

"All right," said Rose, "but you don't know where it is, and you'll never find it without us."

After the exploration they had just made of the island the boys recognized the truth of this remark. They looked so crestfallen that Rose felt remorseful.

"We can get up early," she continued after a slight pause, "and set off directly after breakfast. Oh, won't it be fun! We'll take a lamp and heaps of matches."

"How do you get to it?" inquired Charles.

"You won't go without us if I tell you, will you?"

"No," Charles promised. "It will be my turn to be Chief."

"Well, you can go two ways. One way is through a cave at the end of the island where we went *in*, and the other is down a big hole in the ground where we came *out*."

"I wish it was the morning!" exclaimed Charles. "We'll go to bed early so that it will be here sooner."

"Did you catch many rabbits?" asked Violet.

"I expect we have. Shall we go out and see, William?"

"When I've finished tea," said William. "You can wash up, Rose."

Rose agreed amiably, and said she would also put the babies to bed. So when they had all eaten as much as they wanted, the two boys went out to make the round of their hunting ground.

"I'm going to bed when we get back," William announced as they walked slowly along.

"Don't you feel well really?" asked Charles, surprised at such an unusual decision on the part of his brother.

"Tired," replied William laconically.

They trudged along in silence till they got near the traps, then their eagerness overcame their weariness, and when they found that three rabbits had been caught their satisfaction knew no bounds. Without stopping to reset the traps they raced back to the cottage with the trophies of their skill.

"We'll skin them at once," said Charles, when the junior members of the family had expressed their amazement and admiration. "We shan't have any time in the morning."

William agreed, but halfway through the first rabbit he fell fast asleep, and all Charles' efforts to waken him were unsuccessful.

"It's no good," he said at last to Rose, as she joined them after having settled the babies to sleep. "I'll finish my rabbit, and then we'll go to bed. I don't believe anyone could wake him up."

"Do you think he'll wake in the morning?" asked Rose anxiously. "He had a pain, you know. Perhaps he's ill."

"He's all right—only a bit tired."

"I don't see why he should be so tired as all that," said Rose. "He hasn't done much today."

"I expect it's the change of air," suggested Charles, who would not confess to their frantic search of the island that afternoon. "A change of air always makes people sleepy, you know."

Rose looked doubtful; but as there seemed nothing else to be done she waited till Charles had finished his task, and then helped him get the sleeper upstairs to their camping ground. It was a difficult job, but by dint of much prodding and shouting they succeeded at length in pushing him down to his place on the mats. Then, with many yawns, they too dropped into line.

William was still sleeping deeply when, the next morning at sunrise, Charles crept out of bed, and, going over to his brother, took the brooch of office from his coat, and fastened it into his own. Then he went softly downstairs and out into the open, to have a good look at the weather. It was a glorious morning. The sea was rough; but the sun shone brilliantly, and the gale had subsided.

Unable to resist waking the others any longer he ran upstairs and shook the sleepy children one by one.

"It's a topping morning," he cried. "Come along. Get up. We don't want to be late. We've got to get to the cave. I'll go down and get breakfast. Hurry up, William."

As soon as the children could open their eyes and realize the delights of the day before them, they scrambled up, and in less time than their parents would have thought possible, they were laughing over breakfast. and making and unmaking their plans for the day.

"We'll go into the cave the way we went yesterday," said Rose. "We know that way. We might get lost if we go backwards."

"Whoever thought of crawling backwards?" scoffed William. willfully misunderstanding his sister's words.

"I never said 'crawl backwards,'" protested Rose. "But it may be dark if we go the other way round."

"I think Rose is right," decided Charles. "We'll go to the cave first, and we'll take plenty to eat so that we needn't hurry."

The Seven wasted no time that morning, and in rather less than an hour the little procession set out from the cottage, loaded with packages of food for the day. Charles, in his capacity as Chief, led the way, carrying the precious lamp; William and Rose followed, in charge of the babies; and Violet and Stella bounded about, shouting directions to Charles. At several points they disagreed; but after long discussions with Rose, and many turns back on their footsteps, they eventually reached the "end" of the island from which, on the previous day, Rose had foreseen the probability of "caves round the corner." To their surprise and disappointment the rocks that had been their stepping-stones were no longer in sight. They were swallowed up by the sea.

"I'm sure this was the place," cried Rose. "But it looks quite different, and we can't get round to our caves."

"It's the tide, of course," said Charles. "I wonder if it's coming in or going out!"

"Going out," said William decidedly. "Can't you see the wet marks where it's been?"

"Anyhow it will take hours to go down far enough for us to get round those rocks; we might try to climb down farther along, near the cave."

All agreed that anything was better than waiting for the tide to go out, so they made their way to the cliffs above the caves. There a fresh disappointment awaited them. The cove was full of sea. The little shingle beach was nowhere to be seen.

"What a good thing we didn't have to come out the same way we went in yesterday," remarked Rose, as the sudden thought of their possible plight struck her.

"Yes, you might have got your feet wet," said

Charles, giving William a nudge. "But this settles it. We'll go in the way you came out. By the time we get to the cave the tide will be down."

For the next half-hour the girls scurried hither and thither, looking everywhere for their exit of the previous day, to the accompaniment of many scathing remarks from the boys.

"*You* might have come out of that hole; you're skinny enough for anything," remarked Charles to Stella, as he saw her anxiously peering down a rabbit burrow.

"And you call yourself a Brownie!" exclaimed William. "Don't you know you ought always to look behind you on a journey so that you'll know the way back again?"

"We were in such a hurry we forgot," put in Rose.

The boys sniffed scornfully. But, search as they might, the entrance to the passage was not to be found. The ground was bare and rocky, and the girls could remember no particular landmarks, which was not surprising as there were none to remember. At last they gave up the search in despair, and went back to watch the tide. It had receded so little that to the children it seemed to have been standing still.

"Perhaps it's not going out this morning!" cried Stella.

"Perhaps the moon's forgotten it!" scoffed William.

"We'll put rows of stones where the next wave comes, and see how fast it's going," said Charles.

This occupation kept the children happy for some time; till at last Stella came running back from a periodical survey of the cove to announce that the shingle beach could be plainly seen.

"Then we'll go and find a path down the cliffs," said Charles. "They are so low we could almost jump them."

Several times in the next few minutes the boys announced that they had discovered a way that any-one could manage; but on each occasion Rose refused to let the babies try it.

"I'm sure they would fall," she said.

"They would only roll down, and be quite all right," protested William.

"Come here!" shrieked Stella suddenly, wildly waving to them.

They all rushed to see what she had discovered, and there, on the land side of a narrow rift in the cliff, they saw a stairway that had been cut out of the rock. It was hidden from the view of any casual passer-by, and probably no one before had ever looked for such a way in this remote spot.

"Who ever made them?" cried the boys in astonishment.

"It must have been smugglers," decided Rose.

"Then it must be a smugglers' cave!"

"P'raps a bear made them!" suggested Tony fearfully.

"Come along," cried Charles, as he dashed down the steep stairway at breakneck pace, followed by the rest of the Seven as fast as their various speeds would allow.

"Is that the hole you went through yesterday?" asked Charles in some astonishment, when he saw the entrance to the passage at the end of the cave.

"Yes, that's it!" cried all the younger ones together. "Isn't it dark?"

"I think it was a jolly sporting thing to do," Charles admitted generously. "Who's going first today?"

Everyone volunteered; but it was decided that Stella should have that honor, as she had already led the way once, and therefore was best qualified to do it again.

"We shan't want the lamp till we get to the big cave inside," remarked Rose.

"We couldn't carry it there alight anyhow," agreed Stella. "It's quite difficult enough to get there without that."

"What shall we do with our lunch?" asked William.

"Let's have it later on," cried Charles. "The tide won't be up again for hours, so we can leave it here. We can't wait to eat it now. I want to see the pirates' cave."

"So do I, so do I!" shouted the others in chorus.

The Seven lined up in the order of yesterday, the two boys bringing up the rear. Charles carried the lamp, and he gave the three elders a box of matches each from the packet he had brought; so that if some of them tumbled and lost theirs, there would surely be one among them who had got a box safe. As he said, the most important thing they had to consider was light, so that they could explore the whole place thoroughly.

Crawling on hands and knees, puffing and blowing, the line advanced along the narrow passage. A few yards in, it was as black as night, and the boys both recalled Stella's words that it was "miles and miles long." It seemed endless, though today Stella was leading at a quicker pace, as she was sure of her ground, and no longer felt obliged to test every inch before her.

"Is it much farther?" shouted Charles.

His voice rumbled about with a weird and hollow sound; but if there was any reply from Stella he heard no word of it.

After what seemed an age he felt William scrambling to his feet in front of him, and suddenly found himself in the midst of a cluster of children who were all eagerly waiting for him.

"The lamp, the lamp!" they shouted.

"Look, Charles, look first!" said Stella. "Do you see the star?"

Feeling utterly dazed Charles looked about him, and presently saw a pin-point of light, that he knew to be daylight.

"Are you sure there's only one?" he asked.

"Well, I can't see any other. It's the only one we saw yesterday, isn't it. Rose?"

Rose agreed.

"And there's no light from the way we have just come," she said. "I expect the passage turns a bit."

Charles very soon had the lamp brightly burning,

and when he held it aloft the children saw that they stood in a huge cave, which melted into blackness out of the beams of lamp light, so that they could see no end to it. Sighs of amazement broke from the Seven.

"Now that we have a light we can't see the star," remarked Charles. "I think we ought to mark the place where we are standing before we explore. If the cave is very big it may have other passages, and we might never be able to find the right one again."

Taking off his coat, he placed it carefully on the ground in the corner where he stood. Then, keeping close to one side of the cave, he set out, followed closely by the rest. In places the side shelved away, forming other little caves, but there was no mistaking the main wall, and the children kept steadily along it.

"I hope we shan't meet the *glatissaunt beast,* that Sir Palomides was always hunting," exclaimed William, who had read Malory's *Morte d'Arthur* till he knew every incident in the lives of the Knights of the Round Table.

"What's that?" asked Tony in a whisper. "Is it a bear?"

"No, it's much bigger than a bear."

"Is it a million times as big?"

"Yes."

"Oh!"

For a few moments the children continued their way in silence.

"I wonder where this cave ends?" broke in William impatiently. "It must be miles long."

Just then Charles stumbled. There was a crash, and the cave was in total darkness. The children began to shout out questions, and William called his brother a clumsy idiot.

"Not so clumsy as you are!" retorted Charles. "I fell over my coat. Look, there's the star!"

The children could hardly believe their eyes.

"I thought we were going straight along," gasped Rose. "Are you sure it's your coat, Charles?"

"Yes, I am," said Charles, fumbling about in the dark. "I can feel a snail that I put in my pocket yesterday."

"Then you ought to set him free," cried Violet. "He'll die if you keep him there."

"I'll let him loose directly we get outside," promised Charles; "I forgot all about him."

"The cave must be round," observed William with solemn emphasis.

"Great Thought for the day by Galileo II," said Charles flippantly. "I should think it *is* round."

"Of course you can think so, now I've thought it first."

"Light the lamp, Charles," interrupted Rose. "I want to see."

Charles struck a match. Happily the lamp was unharmed, and was very soon brightly burning. Once more the Seven went round the cave, to make sure of its shape. Then, when they came again to the coat, they lost all fear of its black depths, and began playing about at being smugglers.

"Charles," whispered William. "I have an idea!"

"Does it hurt?" asked Charles.

"You think this is a smugglers' cove, don't you?" William continued earnestly. "They must have made the steps up the cliff and used them at high tide, when they couldn't get here through the cave from the sea. Now why did they do that?"

"Perhaps they stored their treasure here?"

"Of course they did. That's my idea."

"But I expect they took it away again. The cave looks empty now."

"Yes, it does," agreed William, "but the treasure

may be hidden, and I think we ought to have a good look round."

"So do I. We are sure to find something. But I shouldn't think smugglers would come to a place like this. The landing is too difficult and risky. I have another idea. Perhaps we shall find Old Ned's Nest-egg! Listen all," went on Charles in a loud voice. "This is the cave of Ali Baba and the Forty Thieves."

Shrieks of joy from the children met this statement.

"Oh, how lovely!" exclaimed Rose.

"Where is the treasure?" cried Violet.

"Where's Ali Baba?" asked Tony.

"Oh, Ali Baba has been dead for hundreds of years," answered Charles with assurance; "but the treasure is here, and we must find it."

Nothing could have appealed more strongly to the Seven than a real treasure-hunt. They began excitedly to discuss the best way of setting about it.

"I'll carry the lamp," decided Charles at length, "and we must search each crack and opening as we come to it. We must all keep together because it's no good looking in the dark."

For some time they followed this plan, and within

the next hour, they went round the cave many times and came back again and again to Charles' coat. Finding no signs of any treasure they began to weary of this systematic search, and one by one they wandered off, in the dim light to which their eyes had now become accustomed, to explore wherever their fancy led them.

"It will be very difficult to find, of course," said Charles. "You wouldn't expect Old Ned or Ali Baba to hide a treasure in an easy place that any baby could see."

"What about lunch?" inquired William presently. "I'm not a bit hungry; but we don't want the tide to come up and wash the food away."

"The tide's going out," said Charles; "but we may as well have lunch all the same. Shall we all go back and have it, or shall I try to bring it here?"

"We'll all go back together," decided Rose quickly. "We don't want to separate again."

The journey out seemed very much easier than the journey in, and in a short space of time they were all sitting on the shingle beach, enjoying a hearty lunch.

"How nice to see the sun again," remarked Rose. "I'm glad we're not cavemen."

"You'd be very glad to be one if it came on to rain," said William. "I don't suppose they stayed in their caves all day long—do you, Charles?"

"Certainly not. They had to come out every morning to look for dinosaurs' eggs for breakfast."

"Where did dinosaurs build their nests?" asked Stella, who had an inquiring mind.

"Mostly in the craters of volcanoes," said William solemnly, "which was very convenient because then the eggs were already cooked when the cavemen found them. In those days they hadn't got any saucepans large enough to boil them in—had they, Charles?"

"No, certainly not. And no egg-boiler big enough to tell them when they were done."

The babies' eyes grew very round at the thought of such stupendous eggs.

"How big were they?" asked Tony.

"Enormous," declared William.

"As big as a house?" asked Maurice.

"Much bigger."

"Oh, I wish I had one."

"You would never be able to crack it, anyhow," said Charles. "The shell——"

"Don't you think it's time to go and look for the

treasure again?" interrupted Rose. "We've finished up everything we brought for lunch."

"We ought to have brought more," said William regretfully.

"I thought you said just now that you weren't hungry," exclaimed Violet.

"I'm not exactly hungry: but I don't feel that I've had quite enough to eat."

"That's a good thing," said Charles cheerfully. "We've got to get through the passage again, and it wouldn't do for you to be much fatter than you are. Come along. I'll go first this time."

With renewed vigor the children started their treasure-hunt again. For a long time they carried it on with enthusiasm. Then gradually they grew very tired of wandering round in the semi-darkness, and when Charles suggested that they should make their way through the passage inland, and go back to the cottage to tea, they welcomed the plan with delight.

"We can come back here again tomorrow," said William, who would not believe that so perfect a hiding-place contained no treasure.

Suddenly, from out of the blackness of a far corner of the cave, came a piercing yell.

"It's Maurice!" cried Rose, as she and the boys

rushed to the spot whence the cries of distress came. "Maurice, Maurice, what ever is the matter?"

The yells continued without ceasing, and as Anthony joined in the uproar the cave was filled with a deafening noise.

"I'll get the lamp," shouted Charles. "It's all right, Maurice. We're coming."

By this time Rose had found Maurice, and was trying to draw him to her.

"He's stuck in a crevice, and can't get out," she said, and as Charles ran up with the lamp they saw that Maurice was wedged into a cleft in the rock, through which he had evidently tried to crawl.

"Now, stay still," ordered Rose, holding one of his hands tightly, "and stop crying. We'll soon get you out."

The sight of the light and the nearness of the other children comforted Maurice a little, and his cries gradually subsided.

"He's got more than half of his body through," said Charles. "Now, Maurice, I'll hold you tight, and you must try to wriggle out this way. You wriggled in, so you must be able to wriggle out."

With great difficulty, and much sobbing and complaining on the part of Maurice, he was persuaded to wriggle, and after prolonged efforts he was once more free.

"Oh, dear," exclaimed Rose, as she hugged him, "how ever did you get in there? Just look at it, Charles! It doesn't look wide enough for a cat to get through."

Charles moved his lamp up and down the narrow fissure from which Maurice had just been released.

"Where did it go, Maurice?" he asked. "Could you feel the end of it?"

"It's full of pennies," said Maurice. "I got some!"

He opened one chubby hand and, by the flickering light, the children saw two coins lying on his palm. In speechless amazement William took one up and looked at it. Then he gave a great shout.

"It's gold!" he cried. "It's the treasure!"

CHAPTER XIV

THE ARRIVAL OF ROBERT

THE Seven were positive that the two coins found by Maurice were but the first fruits of some great treasure that lay hidden in the fissure of the rock. They crowded round, and each in turn tried to get some further proof of it. They stretched out their arms to their longest extent, they lay flat on the floor of the cave and stretched, they stood up and stretched; but they one and all failed to find anything whatever.

"Perhaps the coins that Maurice got are the only ones left," suggested Rose despondently.

"No, I'm sure there are millions more," William protested. "If Old Ned, or some other miser hid the treasure he would be sure to push it in as far as he could. We shall have to get something with a long handle to drag it out."

"A rake, or some tool like that," said Charles. "We'll go out and look for one, and if there isn't one about we'll make one."

"It must be getting late," said Rose. "I vote we go home to tea now, and come back again tomorrow."

After a good deal of discussion this plan was decided on. With Stella leading they set out along the passage inland—"Old Ned's back door," as the Seven decided it should be called—while the entrance from the cave was to be known as the "front door." Once out in the open again they talked of nothing else but treasure trove all the way to the cottage. The question of food as a topic of conversation faded, for the time being, into insignificance.

"What ever will Daddy and Mummy say!" cried Charles for the twentieth time. "What a lovely surprise it will be for them!"

"We'll get it all out of the cave tomorrow and pile it in a big heap, so that they will see it directly they come," said William. "Shall we go back and get some of it directly after tea?"

"I think we ought to see if we have caught any more rabbits," said Charles, "and set the traps again."

"We haven't cooked the ones you caught yesterday yet," objected Rose. "Don't catch more than we want."

"Perhaps we shall be here all the winter," put in Violet hopefully. "Then we shall need the skins for fur coats. They will be difficult to make because we haven't any needles or cotton."

"We shall have to manage with long grasses, and pointed sticks or thorns. What fun it would be if we had to stay here for a whole year—if Daddy and Mummy could come over twice a week in an aeroplane and drop food and letters."

"It would be jolly cold," said William. "There's no wood on the island so we should never be able to have a proper fire."

"Perhaps we shall find a coal mine," suggested Stella.

"I doubt it," said William, who was steeped in geological lore, "coal is not found in rocks."

"I want to go home to Daddy and Mummy," declared Anthony emphatically, and Maurice heartily agreed with him.

"It's all right for you babies," cried William, "but we shall have to do lessons at the end of the summer, if not before. We've got to have a horrible tutor!"

"I wonder if he will be strict!" mused Rose.

"I shan't do anything he tells us," decided Charles, as they arrived at the cottage door.

The thought of the treasure made the Seven reckless of economy, and they laid themselves a right royal tea. They were in high spirits, and the meal started hilariously.

Suddenly, without the slightest warning, their shouts and laughter were interrupted by a loud knocking at the door. Dead silence fell upon the Seven, as they gazed at each other with terrified faces. None of them stirred. They scarcely dared to breathe.

Again came the knocking.

"We'd better see who's there," whispered Charles. "Come on, William. Perhaps it's a shipwrecked sailor!"

Such an obvious and ordinary solution of the mysterious knocking broke the spell that held the children petrified. The two boys rushed together to the door, and after a slight scuffle flung it wide.

A man stood there on the threshold—but he was no stranger to them. With gasps of amazement the Seven looked at him speechlessly for a moment, and then threw themselves upon him in a transport of joy.

"Robert, Robert!" they shouted, giving him such a welcome as nearly knocked Robert off his feet.

"Here, here, steady on, my hearties!" he cried in

a husky voice, moved out of his usual matter-of-fact outlook by the warmth of the children's greeting.

"Oh, Robert!" said Rose, with a catch in her breath that sounded like a sob, while the others still clung to him. They had expected the door to open to some strange sailor, and the sight of a well-known face brought a great revulsion of feeling. It linked them up with memories of home, and for the moment all the delights of their new life were forgotten.

"Have Daddy and Mummy come too?" suddenly cried Violet, dashing out into the open to see if they were anywhere in hiding.

"No, they aren't here," said Robert. "I came alone."

"Why didn't they come too?"

"Where are they?"

"How are they?"

"Did they miss us?"

Questions were hurled quickly and all together at Robert, and as soon as he could be heard he proceeded to answer them systematically.

"Your Pa was nearly drowned trying to come after you in a boat, and so was your Ma. 'Tis a miracle you're not all orphans. James' boat was wrecked, and then your Pa went round imploring folks to lend him another; but of course they wouldn't listen to such madness. 'Twould have been sure murder and suicide to do it, not to speak of the waste of another good boat. The fuss there's been over you Seven! The whole place was stirred up to such a pitch you'd never believe. Then the Governor suggested air-ships and aeroplanes, and as soon as ever the wind dropped a bit they got one over from London. Of course 'twasn't no manner of use trying to land on these here rocks as we all knew, but I warrant you was glad of the fresh victuals you got out of it. Then this morning I saw the Swinge was a bit calmed down, and I reckoned I might just manage it. So off I comes without saying a word to Matilda or your Pa and Ma, and borrows a boat from my nephew, Harry, and tells him to nip over to the Fort when I'd got a good start and tell Matilda where I'd gone and not to expect me back till she saw me, and that I'd light a bonfire on the shore to let 'em know I'd got here safe and sound."

"You're not going back tonight, are you?" cried William.

"Don't go, Robert," pleaded all the others in chorus.

"No fear," said Robert. "I ain't going back till the sea's as calm as my old Uncle's duck-pond. The job I had to land! Why it took me well on two hours messing about, and waiting for a chance. And where was all of you hidden? 'Twas that quiet and peaceful on the island that I thought for certain you was all dead."

"Oh, Robert, what do you think we've found?" yelled the children, suddenly remembering the treasure which the coming of Robert had banished from their minds. Now the idea of telling him their wonderful news set them dancing with excitement.

"Found? I don't know what you've found. Some pretty good shells maybe—there used to be a rare lot about here."

"No, something far nicer than that. You'll never guess!"

"Well then, I reckon you'd better tell me and get it over."

"The Treasure, Robert! Old Ned's Nest-egg! Pirates! Smugglers! The cave!" shouted the Seven.

"Treasure!" ejaculated Robert, feigning great astonishment, but not believing in it for one instant. "Well, I never! And where may that be?"

"Come along at once, and we'll show you," cried Charles.

"What about a mouthful of food first?" suggested Robert. "I'm fair famished!"

"Come along and have tea at once," said Rose.

"We ought to have asked you long ago. We're just in the middle of ours, and we've got some lovely things to eat."

They dragged Robert in, and sat him down on a stool at the head of the table.

"Well, I must say you do yourselves pretty well!" he declared with a broad grin, when he saw the spread before him. "I wish your Ma could see your tea! She and Matilda would have it that you'd be gone to skeletons, being all alone here on your own, with no one to get your meals regular. But I always told 'em you'd be sure to find the grub, and be more likely to make yourselves sick by overeating than to die of starvation."

"We caught three rabbits, and I expect we've caught three more by now," cried Charles. "But we haven't had time yet to go and see, and we've only skinned one, and half of another, because William fell asleep."

"That's amazing good news," said Robert with a chuckle. "I always said 'twas a useful piece of knowledge, to have the knack of trapping the beasts of the field, but I little knew it would be called for so soon in your case. I'll make a rare stew after tea for tomorrow's dinner."

"Can you cook?" asked Stella.

"Rather! I don't let on to Matilda all the things I can do, because if she knew the sum total of them she might give up work and expect—why, what ever's that?"

While Robert was talking, Charles had got quietly up and laid on the table in front of him the two coins that Maurice had grasped so tightly when rescued from the fissure in the cave.

"The Treasure," he announced solemnly.

The Seven waited in breathless expectancy as Robert took up the two coins very carefully and weighed them in his hand, peering at them in silence the while. Then he put one between his teeth and, to the horror of the children, tried to bite it. Finally he rang one down on the floor, on which it chinked musically and then lay still, while Robert gazed at it as one in a trance.

"Did you get it from your Pa's watch-chain?" he asked at length, still not believing wholly in the confused story the children had told him about a treasure.

"Of course not!" scoffed William. "And Daddy hasn't got a watch-chain anyhow!"

"It's the Treasure, Robert," repeated Charles earnestly. "There are millions of these in the cave

—at least I expect there are. We haven't seen them yet. We're going to get them all out tomorrow. Are these roubles, or doubloons, or what do you think they are?"

"They're guineas," declared Robert emphatically, "and good ones too. Tom, my nephew Tom, has one hanging on to his watch-chain. He got it in Jersey, when he went there last August Bank Holiday twelve month, and gave twenty-five shillings for it, which I always said was a swindle because we all know that a guinea is twenty-one shillings. But he says they're terribly rare, and that's why they put the price up. The man who sold it him told him 'twas a great bargain and worth treble the money. He says it's a case of supply and demand, same as 'tis with fish and such-like."

"Well, they won't be rare any longer now," said the practical Stella. "We shall be awfully rich. Won't Daddy and Mummy be glad? And you can take as much as you like, Robert."

Robert looked at the coins reflectively, and then shook his head.

"No, thank you all the same," he said at length. "I could never keep them dark from Matilda, and if she knew I was rich she would never rest till she dragged me off to go and live in London or some such outlandish place. But no doubt your Pa and Ma will be pleased."

"Do you think that Father and Mother will want to go back to London to live, too, if *we* are rich?" asked Charles in sudden dismay at the idea of such a deplorable result from treasure trove.

"If so we'd much rather be poor," said Rose, and it was easy to see that she voiced the opinion of everyone present.

"Well, now you've found it I think we'd better see how much it amounts to before we decide if 'twould be the highest wisdom to keep it dark," said Robert. "There's no gainsaying 'twould come in very useful, with all you Seven to feed, and find in shoe-leather; and then there's your schooling!"

"We don't want any," quickly objected William.

"Then you'll have to go to sea or emigrate. If I was you I'd get some schooling, and then, when you're full-grown, you can come back here and buy this island and as many more like it as take your fancy. And I'd like to have a look at Old Ned's Nest-egg—if so be it's that you've come across. 'Tis a wonderful find, and the whole of Alderney will go crazy when they hear of it. To think it was here all the time and nobody ever found it till you infants come along!"

With all their enthusiasm restored, the Seven flocked round him, and piloted him outside toward the cave.

"We'll go by the back door," said Charles. "It's sure to be high tide by now, so the cliff passage will be full of water."

"It's somewhere here, isn't it, Charles?" asked William, stopping and gazing round at the bare scrub.

"No, it's farther on," cried Charles, running ahead. Then he, too, stopped and began scouting round. Finally, both boys gazed at one another and grew very red. History had repeated itself. They were as much at sea over the entrance by the back door as the girls had been that very morning.

"Did you girls notice the place?" asked Charles in a subdued voice. "You've done it twice."

"No," said Stella. "We didn't bother to look, because we thought you were so clever you'd be sure to remember to mark the spot."

"You don't mean to say you've lost it?" said Robert in a disappointed voice.

"It's all right, Robert. We've only lost the back

door to it. We can go in by the front, but we shall have to wait till it's low tide."

"H'm," grunted Robert. "That won't be till pretty well on midnight. We'd best leave it till to-morrow. Perhaps it's just as well. We've got plenty to do to fill in the time. There's that bonfire to make, and the rabbit stew, and after that I feel I could do with a bit of sleep."

Robert was delighted with all that he saw in the cottage, and expressed the highest approval of the Seven's arrangements. He declared that Matilda herself could not have got the store-cupboard into better order, and the list he considered a masterpiece. With a few skillful pulls he finished skinning the rabbits and then, accompanied by all the children, went out to inspect the traps. Only three had been left set and, to the boys' great pride, a rabbit lay snared in each. Robert was loud in praise of their skill.

"If I'd only known the amount of wisdom you had amongst you I'd never have risked my life getting across the Swinge to you," he said. "Here you are, every bit as knowing as Robinson Crusoe himself, and to think of the time your Ma and Pa and Matilda and me wasted in worrying about you."

"Fancy your worrying about *us!*" exclaimed William. "You might have known we'd be all right, and that Charles and I could manage."

"You only fell down the well once," remarked Stella slyly.

"That's nothing!" retorted William stoutly. "We got all the water we wanted anyhow."

"Now for the bonfire!" interrupted Robert, scenting a long and heated discussion.

"Can we make a bonfire, too?" inquired Anthony eagerly.

"Of course, you've all got to help," said Robert. "Collect all the bits of old boxes and rubbish you can see around, and I'll cut some dry gorse. We'll soon have a good blaze-up."

With the help of his seven willing assistants Robert stacked up a great pile of brushwood. Over this he poured a little oil to give the fire a good start, and as soon as he set a match to it a great flame shot up high into the air, and a cheerful crackling began.

"Do you think Daddy and Mummy will be sure to see it?" asked Anthony.

"Of course they will," asserted Robert. "You could see all that smoke for miles around, and at night they'll see the flames if we keep it going till after dark. We'll bank it up well before we turn in and go to bed. What time do you youngsters go to bed now? I hope you haven't been burning midnight oil."

"We just go when we feel tired," said Rose loftily. "We never go till we want to go."

"Well, that's a comfort," said Robert with a prolonged sigh of relief. "As everybody here does what they likes I shall follow the good example. And I'm going to bed pretty soon. I want plenty of beauty sleep, I do."

"Do you think beauty sleep really does make you beautiful?" asked Rose doubtfully.

"Why, just look at me!" exclaimed Robert, thumping his chest hard. "Here am I, fifty-one on Christmas Day, and never missed a minute of it yet. Don't that speak for itself?"

Rose looked fixedly at the brown, weather-beaten face, with its deep furrows and countless lines.

"I think you have a very nice face," she said politely.

"But not what you'd call a beauty, eh?" cried Robert, slapping his thigh and laughing heartily. "Do you know what Matilda calls me when she's feeling extra loving? She calls me a clam-faced image. And I says that she and I were made for each other. Ha, ha, ha!"

"I did use to think you looked rather cross," remarked Stella, "but I don't think so now."

"Well, I never! If that's so 'tis living all alone with Matilda that's done it. There's sometimes a whole week goes by and I never sees a soul but her. I almost forget the way to speak, for Matilda isn't much of a hand at jawing, and don't even trouble to answer me half her time. Now then, pile on the fagots!"

Tended by many hands the bonfire had now settled down to a steady smouldering mass.

"We'll bank it up and flatten it down all we can," continued Robert, "and it will still be alive in the morning or my name ain't what it is. Then I'm for bed."

"I'm so sorry, Robert, but we haven't a very good spare room," said Rose, suddenly feeling her responsibility as hostess-in-chief of the island.

"Never mind, don't you worry about me," said Robert cheerfully, "so long as I have a feather bed and an eiderdown quilt I'll be as happy as a sand-boy."

"Oh dear, I'm afraid we haven't got either of

those! We can spare you two blankets though—one to lie on, and the other to cover you up with."

"Bless my soul—I was only joking! One blanket is plenty enough for me. There's nothing suits me like sleeping on a good hard floor rolled up in one blanket."

Rose gave a sigh of relief, and went into the cottage to prepare the guest chamber. In a few minutes she came to the door, calling loudly for the boys.

"There's not a drop of water left," she said. "I expect Robert would like a wash, and we all ought to have one before we go to bed. You must go to the well."

"Bother!" exclaimed both boys together, as they busily stirred the bonfire to make it blaze. "Do you really want a wash, Robert?"

"Not I!" cried Robert. "Don't you bother about me. I'll get my hot bath in the morning—straight from the well. I never wash at night—too much water's no good to the complexion. My skin's that delicate and soft, just like a baby's."

"I thought babies were always being washed," put in Stella gravely, "I know Maurice was."

"Don't you think it's time the babies went to bed, Rose?" inquired Charles quickly. He was anxious to turn her attention from the subject of washing, lest Robert might be persuaded to change his mind. It was so much jollier to play about with the bonfire than to go the journey to the well—a job that both he and William heartily disliked.

The babies had other views on the question of going to bed, and began to protest vigorously that it wasn't time yet, and then went on to plead for "five more minutes." Robert put an end to the ensuing argument by giving a final stamp to the bonfire and leading the way indoors.

"We've got a long day before us tomorrow, I'll be bound," he said. " 'Twill be the first time I've ever been treasure-hunting in all my born days, but doubtless 'tis pretty hard work."

"Don't you think it would be a good thing to have an apple each now?" asked William. "They're awfully healthy things to eat going to bed."

Hearty approval greeted this statement.

"That they are, to my certain knowledge," said Robert. "My old grandma ate one every night of her life, till she died one day at the age of ninety-nine."

"What did she die of?" asked Stella, who always liked to know the reason of things.

"Well, one night she ran out of apples, a thing

she'd never been known to do before within living memory, and next day she just died."

"Oh, what a pity!" exclaimed Rose with ready sympathy. "If only she'd got in a good store! Why ever didn't she?"

Robert shook his head sadly. "We all make mistakes," he said, with a heavy sigh.

"*We* won't make *that* mistake," cried William, with his mouth full. "Do you think it would be better to eat two apples instead of one?"

"Fatal!" replied Robert. "My great-uncle Ernest ate two apples every night of his life till, come to his hundred-and-first birthday, he gave a party, and his guests ate up all the apples he had except one, before he noticed what they was doing. That finished him. He was that used to having two apples at bedtime that one was no bit of use to him. He never smiled again, and breathed his last early next morning."

"But he ate two apples every night and he lived till he was one hundred and one, and your grandmother ate one apple every night and she only lived till she was ninety-nine," objected Charles.

"Ah, but she got more into her life," said Robert solemnly.

"Not more apples!" cried William triumphantly.

"Here, you lads are one too many for me. I take back all I said today about your schooling. It don't seem to me you need to have any more. Now, where's my blanket? I'm going to sleep here."

"But, Robert, we've got a spare room upstairs," said Rose.

"No, no, I like to be on the ground floor. Then I can get up and go out as early as may be, and nobody be a bit the wiser. If there's a blanket to spare I'll be mighty pleased with it, though at a pinch I can do without one."

Rose ran upstairs and quickly returned with two rugs, one of which she proceeded to spread on the floor.

"There now," she said, with a motherly air, "I hope you'll be warm and comfortable. Oh, I *am* glad you're here!"

"So am I, jolly glad," cried Charles and William together. "And what a day we're going to have tomorrow!" added Charles.

With a chorus of good-nights to Robert, the Seven flocked upstairs, and soon the little cottage was wrapt deep in sleep.

CHAPTER XV

OLD NED'S NEST-EGG

"DID you ever see Old Ned, Robert?" asked Charles, as they all sat eating their breakfast the following morning.

"No, he was a bit before my time," said Robert. "But my old grandfather well remembered seeing him when he was a lad. His father—that 'ud be my great-grandfather—used to take him along with him once in a while when he came over here to bring the old man a few stores. in exchange for rabbit skins. He said his coat and trousers were that patched that you couldn't tell rightly what they were made of. And he hadn't washed for years; he just oiled himself over with some sort of grease he made himself—said he kept warmer that way."

"And was he very rich?" asked Stella.

" 'Twas reckoned he was. My great-grandfather had a mate by the name of George. He came over here in their boat one day unexpected-like, and when he looked through the window he saw Old Ned sitting with bags of gold sovereigns all round him. The old man never saw him, he was that taken up with his counting, so after a bit George went round and knocked at the door. Old Ned kept him waiting a while, and when he did come out pretended he'd been having a nap. George had a good look round when he got inside, but there wasn't a sign of the gold; everything was bare, same as it always was. He reckoned the old man had a loose board somewhere in the floor, and had packed the whole lot into it. And nobody ever saw a trace of it again."

"Where did he get the gold from?" asked Charles. "Did he sell rabbit skins?"

"Well, he did; but if all George said was true he couldn't have got such a pile of money that way. There was one or two shipwrecks here, and after each one 'twas noted that the old man crossed over and went up to London with a big box, so heavy that it took two men to lift it. 'Twasn't his wardrobe, by all accounts, and it got about that it was valuables washed ashore, that he was taking up to sell, for when he came home again the box was quite light."

"Perhaps he spent the money," suggested Rose.

"Not he," said Robert with conviction, "for a more close-fisted old skinflint never trod."

"And then did he die?"

"He did, though nobody ever knew the way of it. My great-grandfather and George came over one fine day with a few groceries, and found the old chap sitting up against a rock down by the shore, as natural as life. They gave him a shout, but he never answered, and when they got up to him they saw he was dead. So they buried him, and then had a search for his money. They pulled up the floors, and sounded the walls, and dug up every likely place they could think of; but though they stayed here working at it pretty well day and night for a week or more, not a thing of any value did they find."

"They never thought of looking in Treasure Cave, did they?" asked William, with some pride.

'Not they! 'Twould take a genius to do that. Whose thought was it?"

"I think we each thought of a bit of it," said Charles. "Rose and Stella and Violet and the babies found the cave. William and I guessed there was treasure in it, and when we all looked for it Maurice found it."

"Do you remember, Charles, how we said no one would hide a treasure where any baby could find it?"

said William. "And that's just what the silly ass did!"

"That shows what a cunning old man he was," said Robert. "The chances was all against a baby ever setting foot here. Have you all finished breakfast? Because when you have, we may as well set out on this here treasure-hunt. I'm getting that worked-up and anxious that I want to get on with it."

"Shall we have a picnic?" asked Rose.

"Rather!" shouted the children, and Robert agreed.

"What time do you reckon you got into the cove yesterday?" he asked.

"I don't know the time, but it was ever so much later than this," said Charles.

"It will be later still today," remarked William, "unless we hurry up and get down to the beach before the tide is right up. We might just do it, if we start now."

"I'd like to have a look at it first," said Robert. "I haven't got no fancy for pottering about in caves at incoming tide."

"Oh, that's all right," Charles assured him. "The inside cave is as dry as a bone."

Robert was not convinced, and when he and the

Seven arrived above the cove, and saw the sea already up to the cave entrance, he refused emphatically to follow William's proposal to hurry up while there was yet time.

"No," he said. "I wouldn't go in through that cave now, not for a million treasures. It's my belief that it'll be three or four hours before the tide is low enough again, so we'll set about and do some work. There's that rabbit stew to make, and doubtless there's plenty more jobs that wants doing. And if there's time we'll eat our bit of dinner indoors, and then we can set out empty-handed."

"We shan't come back empty-handed!" cried Charles. "I saw an old sack in the oil-shed. We'll take that. It's sure to come in useful for putting the treasure in."

"And then there's the rake!" exclaimed William. "We forgot that. It's a good thing we didn't go any farther just now, because we couldn't have got out any more of the treasure without that."

Robert was told the full details of the way in which Maurice had found the two coins in the fissure, and then began a search for some suitable tool with which to explore farther into its depths. Eventually William found a long and very rusty rod by the wellhead, which Robert suggested might be bent into a hook at one end if well heated first. The bonfire was still smouldering, and in a very short while was built up and stirred into life, and when the rod had been thrust into the heart of it and made red-hot, it was fashioned into a most useful-looking tool.

Altogether the Seven spent so busy a morning under Robert's direction that they were surprised when Charles returned from a survey of the cove and announced that the tide was going down and the entrance to the cave was clear of water. They had had an excellent lunch of the stewed rabbits, and Robert had been delighted with the appreciation shown for his cookery. The children had one and all declared that never had rabbits tasted so delicious before; and when the meal was over nothing of it remained but bare bones.

"We'll go along at once," declared Robert, "I can't let another hour go by without knowing the rights and wrongs of Old Ned's Nest-egg."

He took the lamp and set out at a sharp pace. Charles followed with an old sack he had found, and William carried the precious rod. The rest of the children had a race to the cliff stairs and, hastening down them, they awaited Robert and the two boys at the entrance to the passage.

"My!" exclaimed Robert as he came up to them. "You don't mean to say I've got to go through that little hole! I'd as soon go into a lion's den with all the lions at home. Are you sure that's the way?"

"Absolutely sure!" declared the children, and without more ado they arranged themselves in their usual formation, and told Robert he could fall into line the last but one, between Charles and William, so that he wouldn't feel nervous.

"Nervous! Nervous ain't the word for what I feel," he grumbled. "I wish I'd said good-bye to Matilda before I started."

"We know the way, and it's quite all right," William assured him kindly. "Look, Stella's out of sight already. Come along or we'll be left behind."

With much groaning and grumbling Robert took his place, and crawled forward as he was told. No amount of treasure would have induced him to set out on such a journey by himself, but with the children in front of him he had perforce to follow. The roughest sea held no terror for him, but the darkness of this narrow tunnel filled him with cold fear. There were many times during the next few minutes when he would have given all he had in the world to be out in the open air again, but with Charles close at his heels there was nothing else to do but to go forward. When at last he stood upright, with the Seven all round him clamoring for the lamp to be lit, he felt ten years older.

They gave him no time to explore the cave, but dragged him at once to the hiding-place of the two golden guineas. William inserted the rod, and began lunging forward; but the fissure was so deep that it did not reach to the back of it even when held at arm's length.

"Let me have a try," cried Robert, his curiosity now well aroused. He seized the rod and thrust it forward as far as he could reach, and then waved it up and down. As it came down near the floor it struck something hard, and a pleasant chinking sound echoed through the cave.

"That's the treasure!" shouted Charles.

"It certainly do sound like money talking," agreed Robert, as amidst ever-growing excitement he raked and poked. "Feels like a lot of potatoes—or maybe 'tis marbles, or pebbles, done up in bundles."

"It's sacks of money!" cried William. "I know it is!"

"If 'tis sacks 'tis precious little ones. Now hold the lamp steady, and I'll try to get hold of something I can haul out. You boys kneel down, and be ready to catch on to anything you can."

He began to work the rod carefully to and fro in an endeavor to rake some of the contents of the fissure toward the boys. Presently a loud shout arose from Charles, followed immediately by an even louder one from William.

"I've got it, I've got it!" they yelled, and one after the other they each drew out a small bag, that even in the lamplight looked old and yellow with age. Each bag was tightly tied at the neck.

"Do let's untie one and see what's in it!" implored the children.

"There's still more bags here by the feel of things," said Robert. "But you're right. Before we get out any more we may as well see they aren't full of pebbles."

He drew a large clasp knife from his pocket and, taking one of the bags, carefully cut the string by which it was tied. Then, thrusting his hand into it, he drew out a handful of gold coins.

"They're the same as Maurice found—they're guineas!" cried William.

"You're right," chuckled Robert. "You've hit on Old Ned's Nest-egg sure enough. Come along, let's see how many more bags the old 'un put by."

Amid great excitement the work was continued. One after the other eleven more bags were retrieved by the children, who now all took it in turns to grope about in the fissure while Robert raked with the rod.

"I think that's the lot," he said at last. "I can feel naught but the rock now."

"I've got a loose one," cried Stella, "and here's another!"

"There's a bag here with a hole in it," said Rose, who had been examining the spoils. "I expect some odd guineas rolled out of it."

"Yes, and that's how Maurice got hold of two when he was caught yesterday," cried Charles. "What a blessing one of the bags did get a bit rotten and burst, or we'd never have known they were there. Are you quite sure you've got them all out, Robert?"

"It's as clean as a whistle in there," declared Robert. "You boys have a go."

He handed over the rod, and each of the children had to have a "go" in turn before all were satisfied that Robert was right, and that nothing more was hidden in that place.

"There's a tidy little fortune in them bags," said Robert. "Who'd have thought the old miser had all that gold stored by and never spent a farthing? I wish my old grandfather could have seen it!"

"Perhaps there's more hidden away somewhere else in the cave," suggested Charles. "We might have a good look round."

"Oh, do let's take this home and count it first," implored Stella. "We can easily come back here again."

"Not much 'easily' about it to my way of thinking," grumbled Robert. "I never want to come along that rabbit-hole again."

"The back-door passage is much longer than the front-door one," said Stella cheerfully, "and that's the one we're going by now. So you'd better prepare for the worst!"

"Oh, dear!" sighed the unwilling explorer. "I only wish we was well out of this on dry land again. Not that this ain't dry, but you can't rightly call it land."

"It's all right, Robert," Rose assured him kindly, "and going by the back door you can see the light at the end of the passage all the way."

Meanwhile Charles and William had been busily packing the bags away into the sack. They were now pretending to stagger about the cave under its weight, and clamoring to start out on the journey home.

"Push along, then," cried Robert. "The sooner we start the sooner we'll get through with it, and the better I'll be pleased."

When at last they arrived out in the open again Robert insisted on sitting down and taking in long breaths of fresh air, to get rid of what he called "the horrors" after his subterranean journey.

"I won't never go back any more," he declared, "not if you was to offer me a fortune. That hole 'ud frighten the French. It's only fit for rabbits and such-like."

"No wonder we couldn't find it!" cried Charles. "Just look at it! Why, no one would ever think it was a passage!"

This was true. All that could be seen was a large burrow in rising ground, and this was so hidden among gorse bushes that at a few yards' distance it could not be seen at all.

"Here, Rose, lend me your handkerchief," said William. "I've lost mine. We'll tie it on to this bush to mark the place—and then let's all go home and count the money."

Rose obligingly produced a handkerchief, and as soon as it was bravely fluttering on a gorse bush the Seven clamored round Robert.

"Come along, Robert!" cried Stella. "You'll catch cold if you sit here any longer. Help me pull him up, you others!"

They took hold of him and dragged him to his feet, and hurried him along to the cottage at a run.

"We'll count out the money in each bag one at a time," said William, when they were all seated round the table with the treasure spread out before them.

"I'll get some paper and my pencil, and jot down the numbers as we go along," volunteered Charles, who loved making lists. "Who's going to do the counting?"

"We'd best count it up into piles of ten, same as they do in the bank," said Robert.

He took out his clasp knife and, slowly and with great precision, cut the string of the bag nearest him. Then he carefully turned it upside down and, as he withdrew it, a pile of glittering golden guineas were disclosed to view.

"Doesn't it look lovely?" cried Rose.

"That it do," agreed Robert. "I shan't ever pity the old miser again. 'Tis a fine sight, and if 'twas mine I'm blest if I wouldn't be a miser myself and gloat over it by the hour."

"Let every one of us take ten," suggested William. "We'll help the babies, and when we have each got our ten we'll know that that's eighty."

"Clever little boy!" scoffed Stella, who never could resist a dig at her brothers, to pay them back for all their teasing.

"Begin," said Robert.

One, two, three—the counting went on till eight neat little piles lay on the table, and still there were more uncounted in the middle.

"I bet you there's a hundred in each bag," shouted William in wild excitement.

"That's about it," agreed Robert. "We'll take two more each, and then see what's left."

"It *is* a hundred, hurrah!" shouted the children, as they took two more each and saw the four coins left in the middle.

"There are twelve bags, and if there's a hundred in each that will be twelve hundred guineas," cried the irrepressible William.

This time Stella contented herself with giving him a pat on the head.

"What ever will Daddy and Mummy say!" she cried. "We shall be awfully rich."

"It's a tidy fortune," agreed Robert. "If you can find enough young asses about with money to burn, same as my nephew Tom, who'll give twenty-five shillings for every guinea, you'll have getting on for two thousand pounds."

"Fifteen hundred," said William firmly.

"Is that so? Well, I'll be bound your Pa and Ma will find a good use for it."

"You and Matilda must have some of it, Robert," cried Rose.

"No, you youngsters found it, and 'tis yours. Not but what we mightn't accept a trifle if 'twere offered us," he continued meditatively, "to put toward our savings for a new boat."

"You must buy it directly we get back to the Fort," said Charles, "and then we'll all come out in it. When do you think Daddy and Mummy will be here? I wish it would get calm so that they could come at once."

" 'Tis calmed down a good bit since yesterday," said Robert. "If the wind don't rise again they may be able to get off to us tomorrow or next day. This time of year 'tisn't likely to blow up again just yet; but the Swinge ain't never in a hurry to quiet down."

"Let's go on counting the money," said Charles. "We want to make sure how much there is. There may be more in some of the bags than in others."

"I expect there'll be less in the one with the hole in it," remarked Rose wisely. "We'll leave that one till last."

It was long after the children's usual bed-time when they had finished their counting and recounting, and made a list of the amounts, and tied the treasure up in the bags again. Their guess had been very nearly right. Eleven of the bags contained one hundred guineas each, and in the bag with the hole in it there were eighty-nine, counting the two that Maurice had found.

"We must go back to the cave again to find the eleven guineas that are missing," said Charles.

"Maybe there are still some loose ones lying about," agreed Robert, "though we had a pretty good search for them. Or maybe Old Ned was working on this bag when he got took, afore he had time to make up the hundred."

"What about tea?" exclaimed William suddenly. "Isn't it time we had some?"

"Time! I should think it is," said Robert, getting

up and going to the window. "It's nigh on sunset, and a very hopeful sunset it is too, and I don't doubt we shall have a fine day tomorrow."

"I want my tea," declared Maurice in no uncertain voice.

"You've been jolly good, and you shall have it in half a minute," promised Charles. "We'll just pack the treasure away in the store-cupboard first."

"Oh, what a pity to put it away!" exclaimed Rose. "I vote we keep it on the table and gloat over it all tea-time."

"Who's Chief today?" inquired William suddenly. "I forgot all about it."

"So did I," said Charles. "That's a good sign. It shows we are getting so civilized that we don't need one any more. We'll be self-governing. Do you believe in a monarchy or in a republic, Robert?"

"Monarchy," said Robert promptly. "A republic may do well enough to the French, but give me a King and Queen with crowns on their heads, and then you know where you are."

"Does the King ever come to Alderney?" asked William.

"No, he don't, more's the pity. It's my belief that the Prime Minister and those sort of chaps don't let him know about us. They want to keep him in England, and they know well enough if he was once to come here and see what a fine place it is, and what a fine set of people live in it, he'd want to settle down here for the rest of his life. What do you want for tea? Speaking for myself, I'm fair famished, and could do with something pretty solid."

"We haven't much bread left," said Rose apologetically, looking round the store-cupboard. "There are only two and a half loaves. Do you think we ought to save some for tomorrow?"

"Well, 'tis no good looking forward to trouble, and as I said just now, if the weather goes on calming down as it's begun, most likely we'll be able to get off tomorrow. I told Tom to tell your Pa to come across in a biggish boat, and I can take you out to it. Besides which there's a heap of flour and we'll make some cakes and scones in the morning, so it don't matter about saving the bread. We'll have porridge for breakfast."

"There won't be many stores left for the next shipwrecked sailors that come here," remarked Charles. "Shall we have to fill up the cupboard again?"

"That's Government's job, and it don't do to interfere with Government. We'll just drop 'em a line when we get away, and tell 'em it's fair cleared out."

"Would you like to stay here for a whole year, Robert?" asked Stella. "I think it would be fun."

"I would and I wouldn't. If I was all alone 'twould be a peaceful life in the summer-time, and I don't doubt I could scratch up a living somehow so long as the cupboard weren't bare to start with. But in the winter I should go clean barmy. 'Twas all right for Old Ned. He had a great interest in life, getting together all that gold, and counting it, and watching over it. He was barmy all right to our way of thinking; but to his own way of thinking he was doubtless the wisest man as ever trod, and that happy he wouldn't have changed places with the King himself."

"I didn't mean would you like to live here by yourself," said Stella with dignity. "I meant with all of us, of course."

Robert looked round the group who were now busily engaged in piling food on the table for tea. Then he shook his head.

"Too many mouths to feed," he said. "I reckon I should have to keep a shop like Peter Dupray."

"Who's Peter Dupray?"

"He's an old man as lives near the Fort. But in

his time he had twenty-seven children. So what did he do, but he opened a shop in his front room? And then he bought things wholesale, and sold them cheap to his wife. 'Twas the only way he could manage to feed them, and 'twas a very bright idea. Now then, tea! And after tea I'm for bed. I mean to be up at sunrise to do a bit of fishing. I've got some tackle down in the boat."

"Oh, Robert!" exclaimed Charles, in tones of disappointment, "you aren't going before breakfast, are you? We want to go to Old Ned's cave to find more treasure."

"Someone must stay at home and get breakfast, and I'll do it," said Robert with a virtuous air of martyrdom. If the truth were told he never wanted to enter Old Ned's cave again, unless some short cut to it were devised.

"You won't go fishing without us, will you?" implored William.

"That's all right! Don't you worry. There'll be plenty of time to go fishing. In my opinion 'tis no great treat, and nothing to make a song about; but treasure-hunting is a rarity."

"I think I could make up a song about treasure-hunting," remarked William.

"Don't," implored Charles. "We know what your songs are like."

"You write it," said Robert encouragingly. "Something with a good rousing chorus. Now then, time to turn in."

CHAPTER XVI

A HAPPY MEETING

THE cottage was very quiet when Charles woke at dawn the following morning. Silently he got out of bed and crept round to wake the still soundly sleeping William. It took some time to rouse him; but once his eyes were open he became as alert as Charles, and in a trice the two boys had tiptoed downstairs, past the heavily snoring Robert, and out of the cottage.

The sun had just risen, the wind was little more than a pleasant breeze, and the sea, though still capped with white horses, was a very different thing from the roaring, racing monster of the past few days.

"What a lovely morning!" exclaimed Charles appreciatively. "I bet Daddy and Mummy will come today. Let's get the sack and go to the cave for the rest of the treasure. We shall be back before the others are awake, and it will give them a good surprise."

William fell in with this plan enthusiastically.

They went to the oil-shed, where Robert had put the lamp and other things, and, having fully equipped themselves, set out for the cave. Rose's handkerchief was still fluttering about like a captive butterfly on the bush by Old Ned's back door.

"We'll go this way, and then we needn't worry about the tide," said William. "We don't want to waste any time, or we shall be late for breakfast."

They were inside the cave in what was probably record time, and then began another search of Maurice's fissure for more loose coins. They poked and raked industriously, and were at last rewarded by finding one more guinea piece.

"That makes ninety guineas in the last bag," said William. "Altogether eleven hundred and ninety!"

They spent another half-hour in raking out every crack and cranny in the cave. Several times one or other of them thought he had found another treasure, which on further examination turned out to be nothing more than some loose pieces of rock. At last Charles sat down with a loud sigh.

"I suppose we shall have to give it up," he said. 'There's nothing more in this cave. I'm disappointed in Old Ned this morning."

"So am I," agreed William. "He might have

hidden things about in other places. Do you think there are any more caves like this one?"

"I suppose if there's one, there might be another; but I don't think it's likely. We might have another look round the island some time. Let's go home to breakfast now."

Robert and the five children had not been idle in their absence; and when the two boys reached the cottage door they were met by the savory smell of frying fish.

"Oh, Robert!" they exclaimed together, "what a delicious smell! Are we in time?"

"You are," said Robert. "I was just going to sound the gong when I saw you coming along."

"Did you find any more treasure?" asked Rose, dancing round them and feeling the empty sack.

"No," replied William, with a crestfallen air. "There's nothing more left in the cave. Only one more loose guinea that we found in the same place."

"Only a guinea!" echoed Robert. "Bless my soul, these millionaires! If I'd gone out and earned a guinea before breakfast I'd have been that excited I wouldn't have wanted to look at any food. You're getting *blarzay*—that's what you are!"

"We aren't!" retorted William indignantly. "But we thought there would be more. And it was jolly hard to find, so of course we're hungry. We've been up for hours and hours."

"Treasure-hunters get just as hungry as ordinary hunters," said Charles with feeling.

"You should have waited for us," said Stella soothingly. "You might have known that you little boys couldn't find anything by yourselves. We'll come with you after breakfast."

The boys snorted; but at that moment Robert began helping out the fried fish on to their plates and, in the rush to their places, further recriminations were avoided.

"Now then," said Robert, "eat your breakfast while it's hot. And eat slowly because there ain't no second helpings. I've divided up the lot. And be careful you don't swallow the bones, because they ain't good for you."

"Will we die if we swallow a bone?" asked Tony.

"No, you won't exactly die. But I'll have to cut you open with my big clasp knife to get it out."

At this moment there was a dreadful yell. The horrid thing had happened. Maurice had swallowed a bone!

"I don't want to be cut open," he cried. "Rose, don't let him!"

He clung to Rose, and it took her some time to pacify him. At last she got him to swallow a piece of bread, "to help it down" as she said, and quiet was restored. Robert drew a great sigh of relief, and mopped his brow with an old red handkerchief that he kept in his pocket for the purpose.

"I go hot and cold all over whenever I hear any one choking, ever since my Aunt Mary swallowed a marble," he explained. "She thought she was eating a grape, and 'twas a mistake that cost her her life—and I ain't going into any details," he added hastily, as he saw seven pairs of eager eyes fixed upon him, and saw seven questions hovering on seven pairs of lips.

"May I ask you just one thing about it?" implored Charles. "Was she——"

"Not a single question," interrupted Robert firmly. " 'Tis a painful subject, and I don't want to dwell on it. I haven't touched a grape since, and I never shall again." And here Robert sobbed loudly, and shed imaginary tears into the red pocket handkerchief.

The babies, now quite recovered from their fright,

told him not to cry; while the elders looked at him closely, not quite sure whether he was in earnest or only pretending. They decided that silence was the safest course: it might be taken for sympathy too deep for words, or lofty scorn, for so pitiable an attempt at deception.

"Do you think we shall get home today?" asked Charles in a pleasant conversational voice. "I want to go; but I don't want to leave here. Will you promise to bring us back whenever we want to come, Robert?"

"That I will. 'Twould be a good camping ground for a week's outing at any time. We'd bring along plenty of grub and go fishing and such-like."

"And look for more treasure," said Stella.

"We're counting our chickens before they're hatched out," remarked Robert. "We ain't back in Alderney yet, not by a long way, and there's a pile of washing-up to do, and all of them fish-ends to clear away. I wish we had our old Tabby here. 'Tis a curious thought, how cats and odds and ends of fish go together in the human mind."

"I wonder why cats like fish," said Stella. "It can't be their natural food."

"No more than roast pork and apple sauce is the

natural food of a man," said Robert. "Yet there's few of us can resist it. 'Tis the savory smell of it, I reckon."

"Robert," cried Charles suddenly, "look out of the window! Do you see anything on the sea?"

"On the sea—where—why bless my soul if it ain't a boat!"

"It's Daddy and Mummy!" shouted the children, and with one accord they swept out of the cottage like a whirlwind, and down to the water's edge. Robert followed at a more leisurely pace.

" 'Tis coming this way right enough," he said as he joined them. "They've took my advice, too, and 'tis a goodish-sized boat. That'll be William Hay's *Sunflower* they've got the loan of, by the look of her, and a very good boat she is."

"I can see two boats," cried Tony.

"That's right. That's the dinghy—that little one tied on behind. I'm glad they brought her. I shouldn't fancy the job of getting you all off in the old tub I came in, single-handed too."

"Not single-handed, Robert," said Charles reproachfully. "Don't you remember how we all helped you off that time when you went back alone?"

"That I do, now you come to mention it. Blest if

it hadn't gone clean out of my head! Still, I ain't never sorry to see other folks doing a bit of work."

The boat drew rapidly nearer, and the children could see a waving handkerchief answering their own excited signals of welcome.

"The treasure!" cried Charles, all at once remembering the great surprise they had in store. "Shall we bring it down here?"

"No, let's spread it all out on the table, and then take them into the room without telling them it's there," said Rose.

"That's a good idea," agreed William. "We'll go and do it quickly now, before they come."

The Seven sped back to the cottage, while Robert shouted after them that there was no need for such haste, and that they might as well wash up while they were about it. He might as well have spoken to the wind. They rushed into the cottage, and helter-skelter to the store-cupboard.

"We'll clear the things off the table," cried Rose, "and then we'll empty all the bags on to it, and make a big pile of gold."

No sooner said than done; and when the twelve bags had been emptied out, a shout of joy rose from the children.

"It looks like a dream," cried Stella.

"Now listen, Tony and Maurice," said Rose solemnly. "Don't you tell Daddy and Mummy what we have got for them. It's a secret, and we want to surprise them. You must never tell secrets."

"Is it their birfday?" asked Tony, who quite understood the necessity for secrets on such occasions.

"We'll pretend it is. They'll love to have another birthday surprise. Come along. They must be nearly here."

Bubbling over with excitement they ran down to join Robert on the rough landing stage. The motor-boat was now quite near, and stopped in its course as they watched it.

"They'll come off in the little boat now," said Robert, in answer to a deluge of questions. "You just wait, and stand ready to help."

"Mummy! Daddy!" shouted the Seven, and this time answering cries reached them over the short span of water that divided them. With bated breath they watched a man get into the little boat, and take the oars.

"That's my nephew, Tom!" cried Robert.

The sea was still very choppy, and it was some time before Mr. and Mrs. Bailey succeeded in joining Tom in the dinghy. Then the watchers saw them settle down, and start to row steadily toward them. As they came near the Seven pressed forward in their excitement. Suddenly a shriek that was not a shriek of joy rent the air. Maurice, who was standing in front of the group, either had been pushed, or had overbalanced, from the edge of the planks that formed the landing stage and, before anyone could move to save him, was gasping and struggling in the water. The next instant there was a shout from the boat, followed by a splash, and the children saw Mr. Bailey swimming strongly toward them. They shouted and waved, and cried out words of encouragement to Maurice. They leant over the landing stage to try to reach him, and Robert was only just in time to save Stella, too, from toppling over.

"You can't reach him," he shouted. "Stand up, and I'll throw him a rope."

"He'll never be able to take hold of it," said Rose.

"Here, give it to me," cried Charles, and before Robert could stop him he had jumped into the water, touching it side by side with William, who had jumped at the same moment. They came up spluttering, and had just succeeded in dashing the water from their eyes when Mr. Bailey reached them.

He seized Maurice, and in two or three strokes was at the landing stage. Robert, leaning over, took the half-drowned child from him and handed him to Rose.

"Rub him down quick," he said. The girls needed no second bidding. Violet tore off her dress for a towel, and Maurice was rubbed down harder than he had ever been rubbed before, while Robert turned to help Mr. Bailey and the two boys.

The boys were not used to swimming in clothes, and they were making a tremendous splashing as Mr. Bailey took Robert's outstretched hand and climbed up on to the landing stage.

"Come back at once, boys," he shouted to them. "Robert, keep an eye on them while I see to Maurice."

At that moment Maurice began to cry and sob loudly, while the girls redoubled their efforts to revive him.

"He'll be all right now," said Mr. Bailey. "Take off his wet things and go on rubbing. Don't stop. His circulation must be restored."

By the time he turned again to Robert the boys were clinging to the posts, and struggling to climb up. Robert let down the end of rope, which Charles had let go long before, and one after the other the boys were hauled up. At the same moment the dinghy was rowed alongside, and Mrs. Bailey's voice rose above the cries of Maurice and the shouts of the others.

"Oh, Arthur, Arthur, are they all right?"

"Quite all right," shouted Mr. Bailey, as he and Robert stood ready to help her to land. "Don't jump till I tell you. I don't want another bath this morning."

Mrs. Bailey smiled courageously, though she was trembling with anxiety. She waited for the signal; then she jumped, her hands were caught by the men, and she was kneeling over Maurice and hugging him tightly to her, while the rest of the Seven hugged Mr. Bailey and each other indiscriminately.

"Well, I never expected such a welcome!" said Mr. Bailey, when the excitement had quieted down enough for him to hear himself speak. "I really feel that we have our family round us again at last, don't you, darling?"

"Yes, I do," replied Mrs. Bailey, smiling through her tears.

"It's never dull where there's children, as my old grandmother used to say," remarked Robert, as he and his nephew Tom made the dinghy fast.

"I'm cold," said Mr. Bailey with a shiver. "Come on, you lads, we must do something to get warm and dry."

"Make up the bonfire again," suggested Robert.

"We've got heaps of rugs indoors," said Rose.

"Then lead me to them quickly," said Mr. Bailey, striding off toward the cottage. He was brought to a standstill by agonized cries from the children.

"Stop, stop!" they shouted. "It's a secret!"

"What's a secret? Is the house going to blow up? Have you left gunpowder lying about? What's the matter?"

"No, no, wait for us! It's a secret."

Maurice struggled out of his mother's arms, and the Seven ran up to the mystified and impatient Mr. Bailey, dragging Mrs. Bailey with them.

"You musn't look. You must shut your eyes. There's a secret indoors."

"Why should I shut my eyes?" asked Mr. Bailey. "If there's a secret I should like to see it."

"Run and shut the door, Charles," cried Rose. "Then it will be all right. You can open your eyes; but you musn't look in at the window."

"I had no intention of doing so," said Mr. Bailey in mock indignation.

Charles had run off to the cottage and now returned. He and William caught Mr. Bailey by the arms, while the rest clustered round Mrs. Bailey, and thus they came to the threshold of the door to the front room of the cottage.

"Open Sesame!" cried Stella.

Charles flung open the door with a dramatic gesture.

The sun was pouring through the window, shining on the great pile of golden guineas till their yellow lustre seemed to fill the little room.

"Gold!" exclaimed Mr. Bailey in a low tone of amazement.

"Treasure!" shouted the Seven. "We found it!"

When Mr. and Mrs. Bailey had got over their first astonishment at the sight of the treasure a perfect babel of questions and explanations broke forth. They had to be told exactly how it had been found, and how it had been brought to the cottage. The marvels of Old Ned's cave, and the passages leading to it, were glowingly described, and Robert's theories of the hoarding of the treasure by Old Ned were set forth at length. Then came a discussion of how it should be spent.

"Shall we buy a motor car?" asked Charles.

"I want a tortoise," said Tony.

"I vote we buy Mummy a diamond ring," cried William.

"A very good idea, William," agreed Mr. Bailey. "I don't know what the laws about treasure trove are on these islands—but no doubt a grateful Government will allow us enough for that."

Mrs. Bailey smiled and shook her head.

"I think we must save it, and send you to school," she said.

"That's what Robert said, but I think it's an awful waste," commented Charles, and the other children heartily agreed with him.

"We needn't bother about school just yet," said Mr. Bailey. "There's Mr. Cameron-Jones, you know, darling."

"Oh dear, he's coming tomorrow, and I haven't got his room ready yet," cried Mrs. Bailey. "We shall have to think about going soon."

"Not in these clothes!" said her husband, who had just changed from his wet things into a couple of rugs. "I cannot understand how the Romans and the Greeks, who were otherwise very sensible peoples, went about in this sort of thing. I think some very valuable and interesting deductions might be made from this sidelight on civilization in my new book—at any rate it deserves a footnote. How they——"

"Daddy," interrupted Charles, "who is Mr. Cameron-Jones?"

"Ah! That's *our* secret—your mother's and mine," replied Mr. Bailey in tones of mystery. "You just wait till tomorrow afternoon, and you'll see."

"I know!" cried Rose. "He's our new tutor."

"It's no good trying to keep a secret from you," said Mr. Bailey despondently.

"What an awful name—Cameron-Jones," groaned William. "I shall call him Jones."

"You can do as you like," said Mr. Bailey. "I wash my hands of the matter. But I warn you that he got his boxing Blue at Oxford."

"Hurrah!" cried William, cheering up at once. "He must be a jolly sight better than his name. Come up and see our bedroom!"

Mr. and Mrs. Bailey were shown all the delights of the cottage, and were as pleased as Robert had been by the children's arrangements. They even paid a visit to the oil-shed, and then walked down to the well.

"Now you must come and see Old Ned's cave," cried Charles.

"We'll change back into our own clothes first,"

said Mr. Bailey firmly. "I can't stand these rugs flapping round me a moment longer. See if they are dry yet, you boys."

"They are—nearly," cried Charles. "They will be, by the time we get them on."

"Oh, do be careful!" Mrs. Bailey implored. "I don't want you to have rheumatism."

"I don't much want it myself," said her husband, "though anything would be preferable to wearing this costume. But we're quite hot again now, so don't worry."

Directly they were ready, the whole family set out for the cave. Mrs. Bailey was full of fears, and protested long, when she saw the back door to it; but after much persuasion she followed Mr. Bailey and the children through the tunnel.

"Oh, Arthur!" she exclaimed, when they arrived at last in the cave. "What a terrible passage! I shall never go through it again."

Mr. Bailey laughed as he clasped her hand reassuringly.

"I am sure you will, because I know you won't want to stop here for ever," he said. "I believe you are really rather enjoying yourself, if the truth were only known."

"Perhaps I am," she replied with a smile. "I

think I would enjoy anything now I have found the children."

The Seven showed off the cave with all the pride of ownership. Mr. and Mrs. Bailey had to examine every inch of it, and their exclamations of pleasure and amazement satisfied even the children.

"Now we must go home," said Mrs. Bailey at last. "I want to get you all back to the Fort again."

"Shall we go out by the front door?" asked Stella. "It's nearer."

"Then certainly we will," replied Mrs. Bailey quickly.

"How's the tide?" asked Charles.

"Coming in, but nowhere near high tide yet," said William. "So we shall have plenty of time to get out that way."

When they arrived at the cave in the little cove Mr. and Mrs. Bailey were lost in amazement to find themselves on the shore. There before them stretched the open sea, waves were dashing over the farther rocks, and seagulls soared and mewed around them. The sudden change from the cold darkness of cave and tunnel to this sunlit scene, so full of life and movement, was almost a shock. They sat down for a few minutes to revel in the wild beauty of it. Then they had to be shown the old cliff stairs, and afterward, as the tide was still far out, they were taken over the rocks by the way the younger children had first come to the cave, and so back to the cottage.

There they found Robert busy frying fish. The treasure had been packed away in the bags and stacked up in a corner of the room, and the table was laid for a meal.

"I thought you'd like a bite of food, ma'am," he said to Mrs. Bailey. "I hear from Tom that you made a pretty early start."

"By Jove, you're right!" cried Mr. Bailey. "We didn't wait to eat any breakfast. The smell of that fish is delicious. I'm famished."

"So am I," smiled Mrs. Bailey. "It was very kind of you to think of it, Robert."

"That's all right," muttered Robert, who always grew very red and embarrassed at any praise. "We caught the fish this morning and I thought 'twould be a pity not to finish 'em up. You children won't want any more after the breakfast you ate."

"Don't try to be funny, Robert," Charles reproved him. "It's ages since then—at least, it seems ages."

"He's only joking, anyhow," remarked William. "He's laid for us all right."

"Well, you *are* in the lap of luxury here," remarked Mr. Bailey, looking at the stores that Robert had set out on the table with a lavish hand.

"We didn't always have so much," Rose explained. "We saved up, in case we had to stay here for years."

Robert put down a piled-up frying pan of steaming fish before them, and they fell to with enthusiasm, some sitting on stools, and some on the floor. The meal was finished with tinned fruits and biscuits, and all declared that never had they enjoyed any lunch so much before.

"Now we must wash up, and leave things a bit shipshape," said Robert. "And then I think we'd best be getting along. Tom and his mate will be wondering where we've got to."

"So they will," agreed Mr. Bailey. "I told them that we wouldn't keep them waiting very long, and we've already been here two or three hours."

They all set to work, and in less than half an hour the cottage was set in order, and they were lined up on the landing stage, while Robert shouted directions.

"You can't take more than three at a time in the dinghy, Tom," he said, "so that'll mean three journeys. I'll come along by myself afterward if you'll give me a hand when I get off."

Eventually it was decided that Mr. Bailey, and the treasure should go first, with Stella and Tony, then Mrs. Bailey with Violet and Maurice, and lastly Rose and the two elder boys.

"I want to get there first to unload you," said Mr. Bailey. "It's no easy thing in a choppy sea, to get out of one boat into another, and I don't intend to do any more rescue work today if I can help it."

By dint of exercising the greatest care and patience he succeeded in getting all his family on board the *Sunflower* without mishap; and soon they were racing through the water, with the Fort getting every moment nearer and clearer.

"Good-bye, good-bye!" shouted Charles, waving his hand to the fast-retreating island they were leaving, and the rest of the children joined in the farewells.

"*Sit still,*" cried Mr. Bailey. "You needn't say good-bye so vigorously, because we'll all go there again some day soon. I must say I thought it a perfectly topping place. Look, I see Matilda waiting for us. *Sit still.*"

The Seven had transferred their waving to the island before them.

"Matilda's been making cakes ever since you left,

ready for your return," said Mrs. Bailey. "I hope you're hungry."

"We shall be by tea-time," William assured her hopefully.

At last they were all safely landed, and the next few hours were spent in re-exploring the Fort and all their old haunts round about. At tea-time they did full justice to Matilda's cakes, and promised her and Robert a donation toward the new boat.

"That'll just about do it," said Robert. " 'Twould have taken us years of saving, and I'm that pleased at the thought of not having to save for it no more that I don't know what to say to you."

"Don't say anything, Robert. Take us out in your new boat. What will you save for next?"

"A few new fowls for Matilda. She's set her heart on some white Leghorns."

"Now it's nearly bed-time," said Mrs. Bailey. "You can play for half an hour longer."

They went out, and she and Mr. Bailey sat down on a rock and watched the Seven as they ran off to their favorite pools. Then they fell to discussing their probable share of the treasure trove, the children, the future, and many other happy things.

"Oh, Arthur," said Mrs. Bailey at last, "isn't it

wonderful to be all together once more? I feel so happy that I don't think I shall ever be miserable again. Now we can settle down to a lovely, peaceful time here and——"

"Daddy, Daddy, come quickly," cried Charles, dashing up at that moment hot and breathless. "Stella has slipped off a rock into a pool. She's quite all right, but it's so slippery we can't get her out!"

Mr. Bailey looked at his wife and, to Charles' great astonishment, burst into a hearty laugh, in which Mrs. Bailey joined.

"Hardly 'peaceful,'" he said, as he got up to follow Charles, "but it's great fun!"